BETTER HAUNTS AND GARDEN GNOMES

(Un)Lucky Valley Book One

MICHELLE M. PILLOW

MichellePillow.com

About Better Haunts and Garden Gnomes

Welcome to Lucky Valley where nothing is quite what it seems.

Lily Goode wasn't aware she had an inheritance waiting for her in the form of a huge Victorian house in Lucky Valley, Colorado. Life might finally be coming together for her. That is if you don't count the endless home repairs, dealing with eccentric Aunt Polly who claims they're both witches, and Nolan Dawson the handsome home inspector who seems to have it out for her, then, sure, life is grand. Oh and not to mention the strange hallucinations and garden gnomes who are far more than lawn ornaments.

If mysterious accidents don't do her in, then the rebellious gnomes just might. With the help of Aunt Polly, it's up to Lily to discover who's sabotaging her new home and trying to drive the Goodes out of Lucky Valley once and for all.

From NY Times & USA TODAY Bestselling Author, Michelle M. Pillow, a Cozy Mystery Paranormal Romantic Comedy.

To the most talented Bailey

To John for putting up with author insanity

*To a wonderful group of women, authors, and retreat
buddies: Mandy M. Roth, Gena Showalter, Jill Monroe,
Kristen Painter, Leigh Duncan, Fiona Roark, and
Roxanne St. Claire*

To Garden Gnomes everywhere, keep up the good work

Chapter One

Lily Goode stared at the beady eyes looking back at her. They were trapped in chubby faces, some happy, some grumpy, all a little creepy. They waited by the large tree in the front lawn, in flower beds that seemed unseasonably in bloom, behind the broken rails on the porch. A couple standing on the front steps like two miniature guards had pointy hats that were taller than their bodies. The female wore a pink dress and held yellow flowers. The male held a sign that read, "We accept." Several more hats poked out of the overgrown front bushes as if their wearers lay in wait and ready to pounce. They came in a variety of heights and colors.

"Welcome to Lucky Valley, the creepiest

place on Earth," Lily muttered. "Have you ever seen so many garden gnomes in all your life?"

"Don't look at me. This is your inheritance, not mine," her younger brother Dante chuckled. His black sweater and dark slacks were stylish and made him stand out in the mountainous countryside. He looked like he belonged in a New York catalog shoot, not standing in front of a dilapidated Victorian house in the middle of nowhere. "Marigold left *you* the haunted mansion that time forgot."

Lily closed her eyes and took a deep breath. Marigold Crawford Goode. Their absentee mother. The woman who one day left her three children on the steps of a fire station in Iowa and just disappeared. Lily had been seven at the time.

Since she was the oldest, it had been Lily's job to protect the other two. Luckily a kind elderly couple had fostered them. Ila and Ronald Whaylen couldn't have children of their own, so they had become experts at taking in other people's. However, by the time the Goode children arrived, they were worn from their years of raising troubled kids, and life with them had been more a case of survival than of family fun. When they died, it had been up to Lily to keep the siblings together for two years until she'd turned eighteen and became Dante and Jesse's legal guardian. After that, Marigold had popped up from time to time, but none of the encounters had made for pleasant memories.

Why had she thought this legacy would be anything other than disappointment? Everything her mother touched had turned to heartache.

The familiar tightening in her chest was brief, and she pushed it down. Those were old wounds best left buried. Nothing good came from digging up the past.

The yellow porch light didn't help alleviate the unsettling vibe of the old home as it cast shadows over the gnomes in the darkening evening light. The house itself stood trapped in a limbo between care and neglect. It was clear someone had loved it for a very long while, but that time had passed, and decay now attacked the wood siding. Purple and pink paint curled and chipped. It sprinkled the ground like permanent snowflakes. A shutter hung cockeyed on a single hinge.

Trees rose gently over a hill behind the house. She'd seen it as they drove up. Mountains towered to the left, and a valley stretched to the right. The mountain road led to a ghost town, and the valley to a small hamlet that barely passed as a town. It was quiet and out of the way, and if not for this rundown house she couldn't afford to repair, Lucky Valley would have made a fine place for a new start.

Lily unconsciously touched her jeans pocket where a couple hundred dollars resided. They would need to be frugal and make it last.

As it was, the house was more money pit than living space. She couldn't afford to renovate. She could barely afford the gas it took to drive halfway across country to get here. She'd most likely be forced to sell the property and hope for enough to cover a down payment on a small place somewhere else.

"Lily? Lily Goode? Is that you? Wait, don't tell me. I see the shine and I already know the answer. Finally we meet!"

Lily watched a vibrant woman come from the shadows by the side of the house. There were no other cars in the drive and she had assumed no one else was around.

Artificially red hair spiraled from the woman's head, escaping a bun. Thick, red plastic glasses framed her eyes. She moved with an abundance of energy, made even more apparent by the bright orange and white of her jumpsuit. It was only after she neared that Lily saw a hint of the woman's age in wrinkles near her eyes. She had the kind of face that could have been a troubled forty or a young sixty.

Lily shared a look with her brother before glancing up at the sky. "How did you get here? Did you... skydive?"

"Isn't it fabulous?" The woman gestured over her outfit and gave a small wiggle. It looked like something a daredevil who jumped out of a perfectly good airplane might wear. "You are exactly as I envisioned you, sugar bee, minus the mole." The woman studied Lily's face. "I was positive you had a mole. The present I brought you will never do now. You'll have to forgive me as I think of something else."

"Are you Polly?" Lily recognized the voice of the woman who'd called to tell her about the house. It was annoyingly cheery.

"Call me Aunt Polly." Polly lifted her arms and lunged forward.

Lily stiffened in surprise and tried to step back, but the woman pinned her arms at her sides with her strong embrace. Strawberry body spray wafted from the woman. Red hair tickled her chin and Lily turned her head to the side. Not exactly known for being a hugger, she wasn't sure how to handle the unexpected contact.

"I wasn't aware one of our parents had a sister." Dante walked closer to the house, out of the woman's reach. He moved with a practiced refinement he had not been born into. Like all the Goode siblings, he tried to erase the past by not being a product of it. "But if you knew our mother, you'd know we couldn't always depend on her to tell us the truth of things."

Polly released Lily and turned to Dante. "Oh, Florus, I would recognize you anywhere."

"My name is Dante."

"You look just like your grandfather. He was a tall fellow too." Polly pointed her finger to encircle his face. "Same disapproving wrinkle in his forehead. You had better be careful or you'll look like a prune when you're my age. Nothing ages a person more than sadness, worry, or cheeseburger pickle pie."

"Cheeseburger pickle pie?" Lily repeated with a grimace. That couldn't be a real thing.

"Pregnancy cravings. Having children. The ultimate worry that never leaves you," Polly explained as if her logic should have been evident. "Marigold had that worry. Carried it around for you four kids like a weight."

"There are three of us," Lily corrected. She followed her brother to the porch. Dante tested the step with his foot before putting weight on it. The board creaked.

"Right. Jessamine's not here with you?" Polly asked.

"Jesse had to work." Lily sighed. Her younger

sister had refused to come with them. She wanted nothing to do with Marigold Crawford Goode or any inheritance left to them. Plus, Jesse's boss never permitted time off.

"I do hope she'll come soon. I love meeting family. I'm from the Crawford side. Marigold was my…" Polly tilted her head in thought, "twelfth cousin's sister's daughter once removed and then unremoved's mother's aunt's granddaughter."

"Wouldn't that make her your twelfth cousin's second cousin," Lily said, trying to decipher the connection, "which would be your fourteenth cousin? Wait, I'm lost."

"I never understood the once removed," Dante said.

"It means the difference of a generation, so Marigold's first cousin would be our first cousin, once removed," Lily said. "Don't ask me how I know that. And don't ask me what unremoved means. That sounds like a bend in the family tree I don't want to know about."

"No, she was once removed from the family coven but then allowed back in," Polly said.

"Of course she was," Dante drawled. He turned his back on Polly and made a face at Lily while mouthing the word, "Crazy."

"So this is the house my mother left me." Lily changed the subject. "You said nothing about it being part of a ghost town when we spoke on the phone."

"That's Old Lucky Valley, sugar bee. We're in New Lucky Valley." Polly paused to adjust a gnome hiding in the bushes. "There you go, Winks. All settled in your new sanctuary."

"*You* put the gnomes here?" Lily asked in surprise.

"It never hurts to have an army of garden gnomes protecting your property, especially a house as magical as this one, and they did so beg for a change of scenery. The salty Maine air is very hard on their skin." Polly skipped up the stairs, moving past Dante as she went to the front door. She patted her chest and hips as if looking for keys before shrugging and pushing the door open.

"I don't know if we should go in there." Lily looked along the porch. A black cat sat on the edge, staring at her with disturbingly bright eyes. "I haven't talked to a lawyer about the property and someone could consider this to be tres-passing."

Polly waved her hand. "Trust me, no one is going to complain about a Goode going into the Goode house. There are two cops in this town. Sheriff Franco Tillens, a cowboy who will see the paperwork as a formality and not care, and who is probably out fishing and can't be bothered. And his deputy, Tegan Herczeg, who has been on the job less than a year."

"On the job?" Dante mouthed, only to whisper, "Apparently, we have the female Lieutenant Columbo with us."

"Columbo?" Lily arched a brow. "The 1960s called. They want their television show back."

"The 1990s called, they want their comeback back," Dante joked.

"Was that from the '90s?" Lily asked. Dante shrugged.

"Come on, sugar bee," her brother said, lifting his hand to indicate she should go first.

"Thanks, Florus," Lily answered wryly. Dante grimaced. "I think we should probably confirm with that lawyer to make sure this whole thing is real. I'm not exactly sure Aunt Polly has all her screws tightly in place."

"No screws," Polly called from within. "But I have a hammer if you need one, and a wrench Herman found on the beach. He insisted I keep it, and I think I now know why. They're in the trunk of my car, which is... maybe in Pennsylvania."

Lily wasn't sure how the woman had heard them whispering from within the house. Dante pointed at his ear and mouthed, "Hearing aid?"

Lights flickered as Lily crossed the threshold. "You forgot where you left your car?"

A shiver worked over her, and tiny memories from her childhood peeked into her mind from behind a closed door. The house was vaguely familiar, or maybe it simply reminded her of another Victorian from another point in her life. After the Whaylens, they'd moved around quite a bit.

Lily didn't go past the main foyer. Time had marched its way over the inside, peeling wallpaper and warping wood. Dust coated every surface, and cobwebs hung like strings from the ceiling and chandeliers. Sheets draped over pieces of furniture though she wasn't sure why since they couldn't protect from neglect and decay. Already this house needed too much work. Even with her brother's help, she doubted they could make it livable because if the surface was this bad, who knew what they'd find behind the walls.

"Spectacular, isn't it?" Polly's voice drifted from another room. "Reminds me of my Queen Anne home in Maine, only flip-flopped around. Your turret is on the opposite side. And the rooms are different. And my house is pink like a decorated cake."

Lily grabbed her brother's hand to get his

attention. "What was Marigold thinking leaving me this? And why? What are we going to do with—?"

Polly poked her head from around a corner and smiled. "Since the late 1800s, this property has passed from oldest child to oldest child. It's just the way things used to be done, and when things are done enough times they become a tradition. But don't worry, Florus, Marigold left you something too."

"My name is Dante."

"Right," Polly said in dismissal.

Dante stepped out of Polly's view and circled his finger by his ear to indicate he thought the woman was insane. Lily nodded in agreement. Polly was nice, but there was definitely something off about their long-lost relative.

Polly went to the stairs. Lily found herself looking to see if the woman wore a hearing aid. She didn't see one.

"Wait, are you sure that's safe?" Lily stopped Polly from going up. "We should probably have someone come out and make sure this structure is sound before we fall through the floor."

Polly giggled. "You're a funny one. There's no reason to fear a little dust and wood groans. A little magic here, a couple of spells there, and *poof* —all done."

"I'm more worried about black mold, wood rot, and unwelcome critters," Lily answered, only to add sarcastically, "but I agree that the only way this place will become livable is if we find a wizard."

Lily leaned against the stairwell and peered up. It was too dark to see anything upstairs, but there were cracks in the ceiling that gave her reason to pause. Where did one even start on a project like this? Structural engineer? Plumber? Electrician? Mason? Exorcist? Firestarter?

"Do you know one?" Polly walked up the stairs.

"Know one what?" Lily wondered if she had been mumbling her list out loud.

"A wizard." Polly paused and glanced down at them. She gestured that they were to follow her.

"I don't think she knows magic isn't real," Dante said under his breath as he turned his back on Polly.

"Of course it's real," Polly called down. An upstairs light flickered a few times as if to support the woman's claim. "Look around, don't you see it glittering on the walls? And in the mountains and valley outside? Like an aurora borealis of magic and sparkles."

"Never mind," Dante said. "She's not crazy.

She's just a hippie."

He sighed in resignation and followed Polly upstairs. Lily took a deep breath before going after him. The stairs creaked with each step, but at least they didn't bow under her weight.

Either she'd been in this house before, or the floor plans were extremely common. Somehow she knew there would be a sitting room and three bedrooms on the second floor as well as a bathroom with a clawfoot tub. Sheets hung like wrapping paper over strange, lumpy presents. She mentally started to dismantle the home. She wondered if the Gothic sconce light fixtures would be worth anything, and maybe the crystal doorknobs or some of the wainscoting. A carpenter might want the reclaimed wood, and an antique store should buy anything she could scavenge. If she drove to a city, either Denver or Colorado Springs, she might have better luck getting reasonable prices. Wealthy people were always willing to overpay for these kinds of things and reclaimed items were very trendy at the moment.

"This used to be a boarding house back when people came to visit the mines," Polly said, leading the way up to the third story. "That's why there are so many bedrooms."

Dante held his arms close to his body to

protect his black clothes from the dust. Lily was glad she'd worn more comfortable travel clothes, jeans, and a t-shirt.

Lily moved ahead of her brother. The stairwell was smaller between the second and third levels. Faded wallpaper had yellowed at the seams. Tiny pink flowers must have looked cheery once upon a time, but now they were just faint and sad. The musty smell became stronger in the tighter enclosure, a possible mixture of old wallpaper paste and mildew.

The third floor was less familiar and by the time she had glanced in each of the four bedrooms, she convinced herself that she had never been in the house. There were antique beds left uncovered, but the mattresses were gone, another bathroom, and a small locked door.

Polly talked about paint colors and furniture, but Lily only half listened. With each new room, she became convinced that Polly's enthusiasm for renovation and "keeping the house in the Goode family" was nowhere near Lily's reality. She couldn't afford to fix a three-story home in the middle of Lucky Valley, Colorado. With the sort of jobs she could get in a town this small, it would take her five hundred years to earn enough money.

By the time they made it back down to the main floor, Lily was sure she was going to sell. She peeked around the main level. The kitchen cabinets were falling off. The stove was large and cast iron and probably only worked by lighting a wood fire. A library still had books, but she was convinced they'd turn to dust if she touched them. The dining room and living room were beautiful, or at least they had been at one time.

"Would you like to see the basement?" Polly asked, going to the mudroom beside the kitchen and opening a door. "I'm not one for basements myself."

"Might as well while we're here," Dante answered for her. She recognized the disappointment he tried to hide. This house could have been a solid restart for all of them, a chance to get out of rentals and into a family home. Their home. A home no one could take from them. But, like everything connected to their past, this Victorian was broken and sad and a disappointment. It was another family legacy they would have to try to patch up.

Lily and Dante went into the unfinished basement alone as Polly waited upstairs. Dante brushed his hand against the stacked stone foundation. Dust sprinkled to the floor.

"I'm sorry, Lily," he said softly. "You don't

need this headache or this heartache. I know you're disappointed."

"It is what it is," Lily answered. "We knew any inheritance Marigold left us would be a long shot. If no one wants to buy it, we'll dismantle whatever we can and rent a truck to haul it off. We should be able to sell most of this junk. I doubt anyone will drive out here for it, but if we take it to Denver…" She sighed, not bothering to finish the thought. It felt like a lot of work for a potentially small payoff. Not to mention, if they stayed, they'd lose their jobs back in Spokane, Washington.

"I'm not sure we'll get much for a leaky water heater." Dante pointed to a corner.

Lily chuckled. "I doubt we can sell this place with that fuse box *next* to the broken water heater. I'm pretty sure nothing in this house is up to code. No wonder it's been in the family so long. They haven't been able to offload it."

Shelves lined the walls of a small, dark room. Empty mason jars for canning food held dust instead. In the corner there were a couple of jars that had something inside them as they sat forgotten by whoever had placed them there. Rust had formed on the metal lids.

"Maybe we can sell this place to scientists who study mold and ancient viruses. Or a nuclear testing facility. Let them mushroom cloud it out of existence," Dante joked. Humor was their way of masking pain. That's what this house was to them, a symbol of the past, of the pain they worked so hard to ignore. Its decaying walls and chipped paint were representative of the insecurity of childhood, the bleakness of those uncertain days. The leaking water heater and dank basement was the shaky foundation they'd had.

The fact this house came from Marigold, the cause of that pain, only made the emotions of the past invade the present.

"The town will probably have something to say about a mushroom cloud," Lily said.

"I don't think the residents of Old Lucky Valley will care," Dante countered.

"We should go to the hotel before we catch Ebola." Lily made a face of disgust.

"There are most likely back taxes or liens on it, too. I doubt anyone has been keeping up on the payments." Dante let her walk up the stairs first. "Make sure you ask the attorney before you sign anything."

"You make an excellent point." Lily had seen enough. "I wonder how hard it is to legally refuse an inheritance. I mean, they can't force me to take it if I don't want it, can they?"

Chapter Two

Nolan Dawson eyed the stack of paperwork on Alice MacIver's desk. Though it looked like chaos, he knew the woman had some kind of system. It was a system only she understood, but it had to be effective. Being as she was the only working attorney in the area, he had spent a lot of time in her office. Enforcing building and city codes was not a dream job by a long shot, and it frequently had him filing legal notices for those not in compliance through MacIver Law Office.

Though, truth be told, more often than not his job was finding creative ways to cite supernaturals within the legal constraints of a non-supernatural world. He wasn't exactly the most popular guy in town because of it. A dirty goblin den would equal unsafe living conditions, and fairies who caused nature to grow at an unusual rate were regularly cited for trees hanging too low over public sidewalks, and excessive weeds. For the last week, he'd been trying to catch whoever had been eating all the vegetation along the north river. He would cite them with stream-side disturbance.

Today was definitely not just another day at work.

Lily Goode wasn't anything like he'd expected. Nolan had been on construction sites since he could walk, and none of the job bosses had ever looked like her. He couldn't imagine anyone but a contractor coming back to save the old house after so many years. It's not like their mother had just died. Marigold had passed away, what was it... four or five years ago now? Occasionally investors would come by wanting to buy the ghost town properties to turn it into a tourist trap. The town was all for it because it would mean local revenue. However, one family trust owned the defunct mines and nearby ghost town the locals had nicknamed Unlucky Valley—the Goodes.

No one wanted to go up against that family of witches. They were powerful, rich, and if the old folktales were to be believed, scary as hell.

And today, they were back.

Lily also didn't look like a rich and powerful heiress. Her wavy brown hair fell past her shoulders, more natural than styled. Her eyes were a stunning green hazel, outlined in black. Beyond that, she didn't wear much makeup. Her blue jeans, t-shirt, and sneakers were not normal business attire. Even he had been compelled to put on slacks and a nice button-down shirt.

And he was staring.

Nolan drew his gaze quickly away from the back of the woman's head. Lily might be pretty, but she was the oldest child of the Goode and Crawford alliance. One family of witches was bad enough, but when those two joined forces, fear ran rampant in Lucky Valley. No one knew just how powerful Lily and her siblings would be, but none of the predictions was good. How could they be? When it was two of the oldest magical family lines in history?

The city officials had tasked him with finding a way to get the Goode siblings to leave Lucky Valley forever. It was why they had voted to expand the city lines to include the house. If only another year had passed, they would have received a legal injunction that would've given them the authority to bulldoze the place to the ground. As it was, all they could do was make it known that the Goode Estate was more trouble than it was worth.

As Mayor Bennett put it, "How hard can it be to scare city folk from the country?"

Easy for her to say. She wasn't the one being asked to annoy the all-powerful.

Nolan stood in the back of the room, holding his files as he waited for Alice to do her job. Lily sat in front of the lawyer's desk with her brother, Dante, next to her. Both were rigid as they listened to Alice read the will.

"To my oldest daughter, Lily Goode, I leave the entirety of the Goode Estate unless otherwise stated within this document. I know her to be a responsible woman who will do right by her siblings."

"Congrats, sis…" Dante whispered.

Nolan inched closer to see Lily's expression. She didn't look happy at the windfall she'd just been given. Maybe his job of convincing her to go wouldn't be too difficult.

"…you are the proud new owner of a stack of firewood," Dante finished.

Lily's lip twitched as if she tried not to laugh. It was the first hint of emotion Nolan had seen since she'd arrived.

"To my only son, Florus—"

"Wait," Dante interrupted. He placed his

hand on the desk so hard it thumped. Alice jumped in surprise as she looked up. "Who the hell is Florus? Are you telling me that Marigold isn't my real mother?"

"No fair," Lily jested.

"Uh…" Alice set down the will and reached for a stack of files. She pulled one from the middle of a pile and opened it. "Florus Dante Goode, born March fourteenth to Joseph Goode and Marigold Crawford Goode." She glanced up for confirmation.

"Holy crap," Lily blurted. "Ha, your name *is* Florus."

"What…?" Dante stood, shaking his head. "No."

Lily reached forward and snatched a paper from the file. It was a copy of a birth certificate. She laughed harder as she held it up. "Your name is Florus!"

"Shut up," Dante ordered his sister.

"Okay, Florus." Lily laughed harder, not trying very hard to hold it in. "Whatever you want, Florus."

"Well, what's *her* real name?" Dante demanded. He grabbed the file off the lawyer's desk and flipped through the pages. "Ha! Lily Cam—*damn*."

"What?" Lily asked, standing to take a look.

"Lily Camellia Goode," he muttered.

Lily grinned. "That's what it says on my license."

Alice looked stunned as if she didn't know what to do. She started to reach for the file but stopped and pulled her hand back. Nolan didn't blame her for not wanting to upset witches.

Dante looked at another paper and mumbled, "Jessamine Rosemary Goode."

"Your name is Florus," Lily teased.

Dante's brow furrowed, and he looked at the attorney. He snapped the folder shut. "We've seen enough."

Lily's demeanor changed. "What?"

"Nothing. Let's get this farce over with. Just tell us the parts that pertain to us so we can go." Dante tried to urge his sister to sit down. Lily didn't budge.

"What else is in the file?" Lily asked, holding out her hand. The siblings locked eyes.

"Maybe we should continue with the reading," Alice suggested.

"Amaryllis Clementine Goode," Dante said softly.

"Who is…" Lily shook her head. "No."

The room became silent, and the two siblings didn't speak for a long time as they held very still with their eyes locked. He wondered if they were somehow communicating in a way he couldn't hear.

Dante glanced past his sister to Nolan as if considering what the outsider was doing there. Nolan was wondering the same thing. This was clearly some kind of emotional family matter.

Finally, Lily looked at Alice. Her tone was even as she stated, "We don't want any of this."

Dante pulled his eyes away from Nolan's.

"Legally, I have to tell you what is in the will so you fully understand what you'd be—" Alice began.

"Fine. Read it." Dante sat back down. Lily was slower to take her seat.

"To my only son, Florus Goode, I leave the trunk in the third-story storage room. It's marked with his name."

"Old trunk in creepy house. I understand," Dante said. "Here's hoping there isn't a dead body inside."

"To my daughter, Jessamine Goode, I leave the key to my safe deposit box. The items within are hers." Alice glanced up. "It's at the local bank. Your sister will need to be present with a government issued ID to access the box. Only she can."

"I don't see that happening," Dante said.

Lily placed her hand on her brother's arm. "We'll let her know."

Alice looked as if she didn't want to continue. After a deep breath, she sighed and said, "To my daughter, Amaryllis Goode, I leave my love, as she is no longer with us."

Lily closed her eyes and shook her head. "Dammit, Marigold."

"That's it. Marigold left her will short and sweet." Alice gestured at Nolan. "Because of a complication with the new city property lines that were expanded three years ago, the Goode house is now technically within Lucky Valley city limits and thus subject to city code. I've asked Nolan Dawson, the local code enforcement officer, to prepare a list of the more serious items that will need to be addressed immediately so the house will come into compliance."

"Hi. Good to meet you both." Nolan nodded at the brother and sister. They both looked at him with blank expressions, and he imagined they were stunned by what they had learned during the will's reading. This couldn't be an easy day for them. "First, let me express my condolences for your loss." They didn't move. Nolan cleared his throat and set the comprehensive list of violations in front of Lily. "As Alice said, there are a few items that are mandatory to bring the property up to code. Though, considering the circumstances of this being an inheritance, the enforcement board has allowed a grace period to complete the non-emergency items——"

"Not to be rude and cut you off, but there isn't much reason for you to go on. I see no choice but to refuse," Lily gestured at the papers on Alice's desk, "all of this."

"I'm afraid that is not an option Ms. Goode. Legally——" Nolan tried to explain.

He'd been warned that witches were tricky with their spells, potions, and magic. The Goodes and Crawfords had been blamed for all the bad luck that happened in town since the first Lucky Valley had sprung up as an old mining camp. Nothing could be proven, but that didn't seem to matter when magic was concerned. Founded or not, the fear was real, and Lily and Dante were at the center of it. He had to be careful or they just might hex him.

"Refuse the inheritance," Lily clarified. She pushed at the pile of code violations without bothering to look at them. The stack slid on the desk toward him. "We went by the house last night. We can't afford to fix it."

"Excuse me?" Alice quirked a brow.

"I'm not a millionaire," Lily laughed. She thumped her hand on the stack of paper. "How am I supposed to pay for all of these emergency code violations?"

Alice shared a look with Nolan.

"Do you not know the full extent of your family's estate?" Alice asked.

"Unless there is some pot of gold inside that rundown Victorian that I missed, I do not see much in the way of an estate. I'll consider myself fortunate if I don't have to pay twenty years' worth of back taxes on it." Lily stood. She leaned over to grab the strap of her cloth messenger bag from the floor and lifted it over her head so that it fell across her chest. The patchwork bag looked like the kind of thing sold at craft fairs.

"Not a pot, but there are the old mines," Alice said.

"What do you mean?" Dante remained in his chair.

"The old gold mines, the ghost town, several hundred acres of land. It's all part of the estate property maintained by the family trust. The trust takes care of the taxes each year. Your ancestors made their fortune when they struck gold. The Goode family helped found the first Lucky Valley back in the 1800s. I have the paperwork right here that shows the extent of your property. There's a map if you want to see it."

"I'll take your word for it," Lily said.

Alice tilted her head and leaned forward for emphasis. "Ms. Goode, your mother essentially left you a millionaire. Of course, a trust is not like a checking account. You can't access all the assets because of the legalities of how it was set up, but the property upkeep will be covered. All you need to do is file a proposal and, if you choose to retain me, I can take care of the necessary paperwork to make sure anyone you hire to work on the home is compensated. It will take some time to set everything up with the various institutions holding the capital for investment, but it's only a matter of legal paperwork."

Nolan watched Lily's face turn from dismissal to shock. What he'd expected was excitement. Regardless of her reaction, her inheritance made the repairs affordable.

"Of course, you always have the right to sell the property," Nolan offered.

Alice frowned at him. If the Goodes left Lucky Valley, she'd lose a big client. Alice could be upset all she wanted. It was Nolan's duty to get them to leave, *legally*. He'd bury them with every code enforcement he could find until they gave up. It shouldn't be too hard. Lily didn't look happy to be there.

"Selling the property won't necessarily give you access to the trust," Alice countered. "There are numerous legal concerns with such a transaction. I can't recommend that option. Whoever set it up was very specific."

It was Nolan's turn to frown at the attorney. "It's within their rights to ask to have the documents examined."

He wasn't a lawyer. He shouldn't be saying anything.

Lily and Dante looked more at each other than those debating their legal future.

"The trust changes everything. It couldn't hurt to give the place a try," Dante said. "Maybe it can be a home after all. And, if you hate it, we walk away and never look back."

Chapter Three

Being a rich heiress kind of sucked.

Lily stared at the monstrous project towering before her and then at the enormous stack of code violations she cradled in her arms. The page count rivaled the length of a Leo Tolstoy novel, but was a lot less interesting. Well, truth be told, she had never attempted *War and Peace*, but it had to be more interesting than... She paused to read, *"the safety standards for automatically fired boilers as adopted by the Department of Boring."*

The attorney had given her a summary of the trust's basic scopes and limitations. Their ancestors had cared more about a pile of rotting plaster than they had their descendants. They could fix a toilet, but they couldn't buy shampoo. They could line the driveway with rocks, but they

31

couldn't buy a car. They could shingle the roof, but they couldn't clothe themselves. They could rewire the entire house, but they couldn't buy food.

Oh, except for the provision that if they had future caretakers of Goode blood—yes, it actually specified a blood descendant—they'd receive a ten-thousand-dollar bonus for baby one, and five thousand for each after.

"And this explains why Marigold and Joseph bothered to have children," she grumbled. Though to be fair, back in the 1890s when the trust had been written, ten thousand was probably a much bigger payday.

She couldn't be sure, but it looked as if Polly had been by to rearrange the gnomes. They had not seen her staying at the hotel which didn't mean she wasn't there, but Lily had no idea where Polly went when she wasn't at the house. More gnomes were along the front of the house. Yellow, blue, and red hats poked up from the bushes. The black cat was back, staring at her from the tree like a silent judge. The gnome couple stayed on the front porch holding their "welcome" sign.

Lily frowned at the inanimate figures. "I could have sworn your sign said something else."

The gnomes continued to stare with their cheery little faces.

"Never mind all that. I don't suppose you know what," she glanced at the stack of papers, "*reduction of friable asbestos* means?"

She looked expectantly at the yard décor, knowing it wouldn't answer.

"No? Me neither."

After they left the attorney's office, Lily had spent the rest of the day calling every contractor she could find within a fifteen-mile radius. No one wanted to work on the Goode house. The following day, she had called every contractor within a fifty-mile radius. One had laughed at her and hung up. So, today she was here, trying to figure out what "*the replacement of minor parts which alters the approval of formerly working equipment*" referred to.

Hearing a car, she turned to see her brother driving their old sedan on the road from town. She shaded her eyes in the early morning sun to watch him. He'd dropped her off so she could get started, but for the most part she'd merely walked around the exterior with her pile of citations and a feeling of dread.

"Picked up breakfast... well, early lunch," Dante called through the window as he parked the car. The driveway was more of an overgrown suggestion than an actual path. Lily went toward the window and took the to-go cup he handed her. The green coffee sleeve read, "Stammerin' Eddie's."

"Mm, thank you." Lily gave a small moan. She didn't usually eat in the mornings, so Dante hadn't bothered to bring actual food.

Dante joined her on the lawn and glanced at the papers she held. "Have you been inside yet?"

"No. I didn't want to go in alone. I walked the grounds. The siding seems to be in decent shape. Paint should help." Even as she said it, Lily wasn't convinced. "Oh, and someone spray-painted a weird symbol and the words 'get out or you'll be sorry' on the back of the house."

"Maybe we should take their advice." Dante chuckled. "Money isn't everything. Let that Polly person have the trust fund if she likes this place so much."

Lily handed the trust summary to him. "Nope, sorry. Polly isn't part of the Goode blood-line, so she can't."

Dante looked it over. "Does this actually say we're paid to procreate?"

"It says as the oldest, I'm worth twice as much as you."

"If we pay it back do we get to leave?" Dante pretended to be serious.

"This whole thing is crazy," Lily said. "I didn't realize it when we were here last time, but the driveway curves around the side yard into the back, where there's a barn garage, a few outbuildings, and a couple of cottages along the tree line. They look like they've fared about as well as the house."

"I still can't figure out what this Nolan guy's problem is." Dante reached into the middle of the stack she carried and randomly pulled out several sheets. "*Tree limbs over a drive must be at least fifteen feet above the ground. Current height is fourteen feet and two inches.*" He arched a brow. "This constitutes the emergency repair pile?"

"He's just doing his job," Lily defended. "It probably has to do with large vehicle clearance or something."

"Right, because this is such a widely used thoroughfare." Dante made a show of looking around the empty country roads and flipped to another page. "*No available parking. It is against code to park on the lawn.* So on the one hand, our trees are too low over the driveway, and on the other, there *is* no driveway." He glanced down to where the rock driveway was overgrown. He flipped to the next one. "*Too many nuisance weeds.*" He gave a meaningful glance to a stray thistle growing along the edge of the drive and then the overgrown flower beds. "*No one shall operate a cattery on premises without a license.* We are being blamed for stray cats living on the property."

"Fine. He's anal retentive," Lily allowed. It was too bad. When she first saw the man at the lawyer's office, she'd thought he looked nice. He had a kind smile—what she could see under his beard, anyway. Normally, she had a good sense of people. One of her foster mothers had told her she had good instincts because of her rough life. Another of her foster mothers told her she was crazy and imagining things.

Lily lifted the coffee cup to take a drink but stopped when a light flashed from behind her. It lit up her brother's face with a pink glow. She turned to look at the house. Another pink flash briefly illuminated the windows all at once. "What was that?"

"Ghost disco," Dante answered.

Lily chuckled. "Come on, funny man, let's see what's going on inside. My bet is on electrical problems. Maybe the place will burn down and save us the trouble."

"I wonder if the trust will let us build a new house instead." Dante lifted the stack of papers from her to carry them.

"No. Only the current structures—the house, maybe the barn, shed, and cottages." She led the way up the porch. The door cracked opened with a small nudge.

"I like your security system," Dante teased.

"You're in charge of installing the locks. Thank you for volunteering." Lily was really glad her brother had come to Colorado with her. Without his smart-mouthed support, she would have been a mess.

"Hey, seriously, all jokes aside." Dante stopped her from going in. "Forget those contractors. Who cares if they won't come out here and help us? We'll make this place great. It'll be ours. We'll figure it out."

Lily nodded. "A home. *Our* home. A place no one can take away from us."

"Or make us leave." Dante opened the door all the way.

Lily lifted the coffee to her lips and took a sip.

She wasn't sure if it was the grainy, bitter flavor of the coffee, or the sight that greeted her, but the horrible liquid spewed from her lips.

Droplets landed on the wood floor—the *clean* wood floor.

"I thought you didn't come inside," Dante said. "How did you do all of this work?"

"I didn't." Lily stepped along the front hall. The sheets had been pulled from the furniture. The room had been dusted and cleaned. Though clearly an antique, the Gothic-inspired chest next to the stairs looked as if it would double as a bench. "This place was condemnable, right? I mean, I didn't hallucinate that?"

"No, but you have coffee on your chin," Dante answered.

Lily swiped the back of her hand over her mouth. "This is the worse coffee I've ever tasted, by the way."

Dante chuckled. "I know. I threw mine out already. It's vile."

"You ass," Lily grumbled as she set the cup down on the chest.

"Hey, you told me if I ate a spider I'd become a superhero," he countered.

"We were kids, and spiders probably taste better than whatever that is." Lily pointed at the cup. "Expect payback, spider boy."

The lights were on and didn't flicker. Wallpaper no longer curled along the edges as if someone had rehung it. Wood floors gleamed— not just polished, but sanded and re-stained. The house was nothing like they'd first seen. Lily wasn't about to complain, but she couldn't figure out how it had gone from a nightmare to livable in only a few days.

As if to provide an answer, the pink light flashed several times, coming from upstairs.

"That's not arcing electricity." Dante set the stack of papers next to the cup.

"Did we step into an alternate dimension?" Lily leaned to look up the stairs. Nerves caused her stomach to flutter and tighten. For some reason she couldn't fathom, she was scared of investigating the light. Each flash tried to stir deep memories, and she forcibly refused to give them attention.

"*Bip. Bap. Twiddle-diddle-dap.* No job is too big for Polly's Perfectly Magical Mystical Maids, Mops, and Lollipops." Polly's voice drifted down from above, followed by several more flashing pink lights. "Oh, drat! I forgot the lollipops."

"Polly?" Lily called.

"I'm almost done," Polly answered. "I'll be right down. Go introduce yourself to Herman in the dining room. He's been eager to meet you."

"She must know a contractor named Herman," Dante said. "She said something about him finding a wrench in her trunk when we first arrived."

"Oh, bless her," Lily whispered in relief. "Now I don't have to learn how to replace a water heater."

"*Bippity, bappity, himble-bimble.*" Polly's soft voice drifted down.

"That woman is nuttier than a Christmas

fruitcake." Dante led the way through the lower level looking for Herman. First he took them right, past the stairs into the library. The books no longer appeared at the point of disintegration and the strange musty smell was gone. Several antique chairs with striped cushion seats surrounded a round table. A writing desk was against a wall, the drawers closed with a key in the lock, inviting anyone to look inside.

As they moved through the rooms, she couldn't help but stare in amazement. They were all as pristine as the entryway. To the left of the stairs was a living room. The red and gold velvet couch had sloped seat backs, wooden scroll legs, and armrests. It matched the chair next to it. The fireplace mantel was carved from stone. They didn't go inside as they moved down the hallway.

Also to the left, the dining room table had been uncovered. Its stately lines looked as if it could seat fourteen people easily. Matching chairs were placed around it, except for one of the chairs that lay on its side against the wall with a broken leg. A purple-hatted gnome statue was placed next to it, as if guarding the furniture. He held a red mushroom in his hand.

Someone had placed a plastic, blue, children's swimming pool in the middle of the table.

She frowned, not sure that was the best idea for the wood finish.

Lily glanced inside to find a single lobster floating along the bottom. Water filled the pool. A piece of material clung to the side rim. It appeared to be a doll hat.

"I guess we know what we're having for dinner," Dante joked.

If she wasn't mistaken, the lobster actually turned to look at her brother.

Thump. Thump. Thump.

"I think I hear someone at the door." Lily didn't take her eyes off the lobster.

"I didn't hear anything, but I'll look. Maybe it's Herman." He moved to leave the way they came. "You check the kitchen and basement."

"Herman?" Lily called. She walked toward the kitchen and looked in. No one was there, but the room was mysteriously as clean as the rest of the house. However, the appliances still looked old and would have to be replaced. On the left, the kitchen doorway led back to the empty living room, so she turned away to check the basement off the mudroom. It was dark when she peeked down, so she didn't bother searching farther.

She went back to the dining room, only to find the lobster had somehow climbed out of his pool and was standing on the edge of the table, watching her. Little watery drops followed where he had walked.

Lily bit her lip, not wanting to touch the crustacean, but also not wanting to see it fall over the side. She slowly reached out her hand, keeping an eye on its pinchers for aggression. It didn't move, and she was able to lift the creature off the table and back toward the pool.

"Oh, I just knew you would make friends." Polly clapped.

Lily jumped slightly in surprise but managed to place the lobster in the water.

Polly wore a lime-green dress with a white apron. The skirt flared out around her legs, showing a thickly layered pink petticoat beneath. Peasant sleeves puffed up around her upper arms. Her red hair was pulled into a bun.

"Was he being naughty?" Polly went to the lobster and pointed at it. "Herman, you need to behave yourself. You know you get grouchy if you don't get your daily water time."

"I didn't see anyone." Dante appeared behind Polly. "Fabulous dress."

"Thank you, Florus." Polly grinned. "I was just thinking I need to buy one for your sister. Is gray the only color shirt she owns? We really need to liven up her wardrobe."

"Dante, meet Herman." Lily motioned toward the lobster.

To her brother's credit, he held back his laughter. "Pleasure to meet——"

Herman quickly turned away as if purposefully ignoring Dante.

"Oh, that's peculiar. He doesn't like you." Polly eyed Dante. "We'll have to get to the bottom of this mystery."

"Dante did threaten to eat him," Lily tattled.

"Florus Dante Goode," Polly scolded with a shake of her finger. "Apologize to Herman at once."

"My apologies, sir." Dante gave a mocking bow to the crustacean.

"If that's Herman, who fixed the house?" Lily motioned around. "I called every contractor I could find and none of them would touch this place."

"So much power in the walls," Polly answered. "Can't you feel it tingling in your toes? I forgot how special this place was. They pulled it from the mines you know, the old power source."

The strange thing was, Lily *did* feel something. She wouldn't call it tingling, but it was a familiar pull. She heard the sound of footsteps overhead, and then laughter. "Who is that? Is someone else here?"

"I didn't hear anything," Dante answered.

Thump. Thump. Thump.

"I swear someone is knocking," Lily insisted.

"Old houses are full of old noises," Polly dismissed.

"Hey, Polly." Lily grabbed the woman by the shoulders and gently forced her to look at her. "I need a straight answer. What do you know about this place? Have we been here before? Like when we were kids?"

"Of course you have, sugar bee. All Goodes are born in this house. It's the way it's been since the house was built, with the bones of the old country and the wood of the new." Polly patted the hands on her shoulders. "You're so far behind of being ahead. It's no wonder you've been drifting. But don't you worry. Aunt Polly is here now, and I'm staying as long as I'm needed to help you find your way."

Polly was moving in with them?

"Don't you have a home you need to get back to?" Dante asked.

"This is what Marigold would have wanted," Polly said. "Don't you worry about me. I'm always where I'm supposed to be."

Lily's hands trembled, and she pulled them away from the woman. "I appreciate that you had some kind of friendship with my mother, but what *you* feel for her, and what we, as her children, feel for her are very different emotions. It took me a long time to come to terms with what I remember, the pieces we all remember."

Lily glanced up at Dante for confirmation. He crossed his arms over his chest and didn't speak. They didn't like talking about the past, especially not to strangers, but Polly needed to know. The woman needed to stop acting like Marigold Crawford Goode was a fit mother and a decent person who blessed them with this great gift.

"My mother wasn't well. She did things and said things that made little sense. Her moods were dramatic ups and downs. We're pretty sure she might have been bipolar. Or it could have just been the drugs she was on. At the time, I didn't realize fully what we were doing, but she used to drive us down to scary parts of various towns and leave us in the car while she scored. She'd leave desperate and angry, only to return neglectful and dazed. Abandoning us at that fire station, for as awful as it sounds, was probably the best thing she ever did for us."

Polly's countenance fell from the jovial expression she had carried each time they saw her to one of sadness. "I cannot change the things you think you know, nor can I change the feelings you carry, but I *can* say that no one is perfect, and some things cannot be seen with certain eyes."

"Thank you," Lily said, though she wasn't one-hundred percent sure that meant Polly understood their stance on the matter.

"So it is time we changed your vision." Polly lifted a finger and looked around the dining room. Seeing the gnome statue, she sighed. "Lugwick, what are you doing in here? I thought I left you in the garden. Herman cannot play with you. Last time, you kept him out all night."

"Polly, you do know they're not real, right?" Lily asked, concerned.

Polly leaned over and picked up the statue. She handed it over to Lily. "Feels real to me."

Lily cradled the gnome in her arms.

"Uh, you might not want to put Lugwick's face there." Polly motioned to where the gnomes head pressed against her chest. "He develops crushes easily."

Lily turned him around to face Polly. "You never said who cleaned up the house. Did you hire a crew to come in?"

"Just me and the gnomes. Well, and the ghosts, though I think we can all agree they haven't been lending a hand around here." Polly chuckled.

"You cleaned all of this by yourself?" Dante asked in surprise.

"It wasn't hard. I just waved my magic finger, pointed and bapped, wiggled and—"

Polly's words were cut off as a spark of pink erupted from the tip of her finger and shot across the room. It wrapped around the broken chair and the wood grew a new leg to replace the damaged one.

The woman gasped and then giggled. "Misfire. Sorry. I guess it wasn't done. See what I mean? So much energy in these walls. I bet you couldn't do that in Washington. I know I couldn't in Maine. Not as powerful as that."

"How…?" Dante whispered in shock.

"What just happened?" Lily held the gnome closer and stepped away from the woman. The sound of footsteps echoed above them, but she ignored it. "How did you do that?"

"Haven't you been paying attention, sugar bee? I told you. This place is magic. You act as if you've never seen a spell before." Polly took the repaired chair and placed it by the table before pointing at the broken leg on the floor. "You can go now."

The leg disappeared.

"How…?" Dante repeated a second time.

"Shut your mouth, Florus, or the ghosts will

get in," Polly warned. "The disembodied are always looking to hitch a ride in the right vessel."

Dante snapped his mouth shut.

Lily's heart beat a little too quickly. She stared at Polly's hand. "I don't understand."

"Darlings, the Crawfords and Goodes come from a long line of witches. Surely you saw your mother casting a few spells? And you can't tell me you've never shown signs of your true natures?" Polly went toward Lily and took the gnome from her. "I suspect it will erupt much stronger in you, now that you're back where you belong."

Before Lily could respond, Polly walked out of the dining room.

"Tell me I'm dreaming," Dante said, "or did the mentally unstable hippie just tell us we're witches?"

"Oh, delicious, someone brought Stammerin' Eddie's. Best coffee in town," Polly said.

"I think that answers your question as to her sanity." Lily glanced out the doorway to where Polly placed the gnome on the chest by the coffee cup. She backed away. "If she thinks that's good coffee, she's definitely not to be trusted."

Lily started to motion toward the back door through the kitchen. If they ran, they could most likely make it to the car. Was that overreacting? It felt like maybe she was overreacting. Polly hadn't threatened them.

"The gnomes will take care of the weeds and trimmings," Polly called. "They're called garden gnomes for a reason."

"Is she rifling through the stack of citations?"

Dante stared at the repaired chair, slowing reaching to touch it.

"Go get those citations from her, so they aren't lost." Lily pulled out a chair at the dining table, away from the magically fixed one. "We should sit down and go through them to make a plan."

"I'm not going near scary-finger lady," Dante denied. He made no move to leave. "She has to be crazy, right? I mean, witches?"

"I know it's—*whatever*—but you saw what happened."

"Shared hallucination caused by a rare mold growing in the walls?"

Lily took a deep breath. "You have to admit it makes sense." Instead of taking a seat, she went back to the doorway to keep an eye on Polly who was still rifling through the papers. "Do you remember when we were little, before mom went off the deep end? The games we used to play? Our dolls walked on their own."

"We were imaginative," Dante said.

"They flew," Lily countered.

"We pretended they flew. Jesse threw them."

"Suellen Grace?"

"Imaginary friend."

"Or ghost. We know what we saw. We all said we saw the same thing."

"The memories of children are not reliable. You remember what that counselor said to Ila when she took us in? We made things up as a way of coping with an unstable home environment. We were isolated. Our mother was mentally unstable." Dante's voice rose in irritation. "We'd been living in a car."

"And the sparkles shooting out of Polly's finger?" Lily kept her voice low, not wanting to be overheard. What she was saying felt ridiculous. "What if we weren't just imagining? What if the things we saw were real?"

"What if they were?" Dante countered. "All it means is our family is more screwed up than we thought."

Lily studied the tip of her finger. Pointing it at the far wall, she said, "*Bippity-ah-pappy-dappy-doodly-doo?*"

Nothing happened.

"Oh dear, you're not making any sense, sugar bee." Polly appeared in the doorway. She placed the stack of papers on the table. "You didn't drink any leftover potions out of my purse, did you? They have side effects. You really shouldn't drink things if you don't know what they do."

"No, you said we were witches, so I was," Lily pointed her finger, flicking her hand when nothing happened, "witching."

"By speaking gibberish?" Polly laughed. "Magic doesn't work like that. You have to have intent and focus, but not think about it."

"But you…" Lily frowned.

"You can't just *bippity-bap* with your *dipple-stack*." Polly shook her head as if that was the most logical statement on Earth.

"I don't think those are real words," Dante said. He sat on the chair Lily had pulled out and slid the stack before him.

"They're real sounds coming out of my real mouth." Polly reached to slide the stack away from him. "These can wait. I think it's time you learned what you can really do."

Chapter Four

"I don't understand." Polly shook her head. Though it appeared she spoke to a gnome statue caring a gnome baby on the side lawn, her words were about Dante and Lily. "You can't do anything. It's like you're…" Polly lifted Dante's arm and jiggled it. "Not magical."

"I told you this was insane," Dante dismissed. "I think I'd know if I had magic powers."

Lily agreed with her brother. She found the whole situation to be insane. She had a hard time thinking of this giant Victorian as hers. It didn't feel like anything she'd own. It felt like an antique store, or a kitschy bed and breakfast that couples stayed at while on vacation. The furniture was beautiful but belonged in a Jane Austen novel. Lily was more of a Bohemian girl with a farmhouse style—weathered tables, decorative scarves, paintings with strange sayings done by amateur artists. This house might be vaguely familiar, but it wasn't her home. If she had lived there, it was when she was a toddler. The only home she remembered with Marigold was in the car, and maybe squatting in a trailer before that.

Lily was inclined to agree with her brother. They weren't witches. If they had some ability, it would have surely come up before now.

They'd been attempting to use their magic all afternoon but no matter how hard they tried, they couldn't mimic any of Polly's tricks. It was clear the woman had some special gifts. She grew flowers where there had been only rock, swept dust and paint peels across the porch with a hovering gesture of her hand, and shot sparkles out of her fingertips.

"And another thing, talking to the stupid gnomes is creepy." Dante's blood sugar was low from not eating which always made him more irritable than usual.

"He doesn't mean—" Lily tried to soften her brother's behavior, but Polly interrupted her.

"Now, you listen here, Mr. Grumpy Pants. I understand you're having a hard time and I'm willing to give you leeway, but don't think for a moment I won't swat your bottom if you don't show a little more respect to those trying to help you."

Dante lowered his head. "You're right. I apologize, Polly."

"And...?" Polly prompted.

"And, I will try to be more respectful to you and appreciate the work you're doing for us," Dante added.

"And...?"

"Um?" Dante glanced at Lily. She didn't help her brother out.

"Don't you think you owe the gnomes an apology?" Polly gestured toward a gnome by the tree which looked to be sitting on a toilet with his pants around his ankles, reading a paper.

Dante again looked at her, and Lily just shrugged before motioning toward the toilet gnome.

"I'm sorry, toilet gnome," Dante said.

"Harold," Polly supplied.

"I'm sorry, Harold. I hope I didn't disturb your, ah, private business... that you're doing... out in public."

"That's better, Florus." Polly nodded. "He accepts your apology and asks that you stop staring at him."

"Maybe the magic skipped a generation," Lily said. On the surface, being magical sounded like fun, but life had taught her that reality rarely lived up to expectations.

"Why would it do that?" Polly patted Lily's shoulder as if to say, *"That's adorable, you silly child."*

"Then we're just not meant to use it." Lily stretched her arms over her head. "We've been at this for hours. Dante, are you about ready to head back into town to get something to eat?"

"You can't go," Polly said.

"We'll be back in the morning," Lily assured her. "I'm going to make a list of the supplies we need for tomorrow to knock some things off that list of citations."

"No, I mean, you can't go back to the hotel," Polly clarified. "I told them to check you out of your room. You live here now. Why would you stay in a hotel when you own a perfectly fine house? Plus, the hotel is about to become home to a family of mice that a very precocious five-year-old keeps as pets and is about to set free."

Lily stiffened and automatically turned her attention toward the three-story Victorian. "But, our bags…"

"Already in your rooms," Polly said. "I put you close to me, Florus. I wanted to listen in case Herman got any ideas during the night. He doesn't like you."

Dante made a little choking noise.

"So, you are planning on living here, too?" Lily asked. "In this house?"

"Of course. I'd never abandon you in your time of need." Polly skipped around the side of the house toward the front. Her square-dancing petticoat swished back and forth under her skirt. Lily and Dante were slower to follow. When they turned the corner, Polly was already on the porch going inside. "I think the gnomes are trying to tell you something. Hurry!"

Lily took a deep breath. After foster and group homes, she had never desired a roommate other than her siblings. She wasn't sure how she felt about Polly moving in but didn't think it polite to kick her out. It could be the woman had nowhere else to go, and she was family. Lily was not like her mother. She would never turn her back on family.

Polly ran up the stairs. Lily saw a gnome with a green hat placed on the bottom step. She moved past him. A second gnome stood near the top with his hands on his hips.

"Lily, I'm serious," Dante said, "if you let Polly stay, we need to find a way to get rid of these gnomes or we're going to have to rename this place the Garden Gnome Bed and Breakfast."

They followed the trail of gnome statues to the third floor where Polly waited for them. A gnome in a green dress holding a bouquet of blue flowers stood next to the small locked door near the top of the stairs.

"What now?" Lily asked.

Polly lifted the gnome out of the way and set her aside on the floor. "You should look in there."

Dante jiggled the knob, showing it was locked. "Do you have a key?"

"Oh, right, you have no magic." Polly ran her hand over the door and then threw her shoulders back as she spread her arms wide. "I command you door to open!"

Dante shook the lock. It still didn't open.

"Is that a spell?" Lily asked.

Polly laughed. "No. Just theatrics. You two seemed to want a big production. She reached for the knob and turned it. The door opened as if it had been unlocked the whole time. "I will leave you two to look. I'm expecting a delivery." Polly disappeared down the stairs, her steps sounding more like hops as she left them alone.

"I hope the delivery is for mattresses. I don't remember any of the rooms having them," Lily said.

"It's probably a shipment of refugee gnomes seeking sanctuary." Dante picked up the green-dressed statue and turned her so she faced the other direction.

The room was dark, and Lily pulled out her phone to shine her flashlight app. The ceiling was high enough for her to stand but low enough to make her feel claustrophobic. There wasn't much to look at, but she did notice a trunk shoved against the far corner.

"Didn't the lawyer say something about your inheritance being in a trunk in the upstairs storage area?" Lily asked.

"Yeah." Dante had never mentioned wanting to find it.

"I think this is it." Lily gestured that he should go inside.

Dante looked as if he might refuse but finally ducked his head and went in. He started to reach for it but then stopped and jerked back.

"I think something is alive in there," he whispered. "I hear scratching."

Lily leaned into the room but didn't go all the way in. "Stop avoiding. I don't hear anything. That thing has been sealed up for who knows how long. There is no way a living creature would survive in there."

"Rats," Dante quipped.

Lily swept her light over the floor. "I don't see any droppings. I think you're safe. Just open it."

"Whatever is in here won't change anything," Dante said.

"Florus, I think things have already changed for us. There is no going back. We can't ignore the present for the comfort of the familiar past." Lily moved the light so it spotlighted the trunk. "Now open that damned thing."

"I hope you know you're starting to sound a lot like Polly," Dante grumbled.

"Bite me."

Chapter Five

Nolan wasn't sure what he was doing parked at the end of the driveway leading to the Goode home, but the strange note scribbled on pink floral paper had been intriguing. It wasn't signed, but who else could it be from? Lily Goode was the only one who had a reason to ask him to come over.

Typically, Nolan would throw on a shirt, jeans, and work boots when he went on site for inspections. Everyone in town knew him, knew he was covered in dirt from being out on a job more often than not, knew he didn't always trim his beard, knew he only wore a suit if there was a funeral. However, today he'd tidied his beard, put on a clean button-down shirt with his best pair of jeans, and slicked back his hair so it was out of his face. There was no time for a haircut, but at least it was manageable.

Lily Goode.

He wasn't supposed to be attracted to her. The town wanted the Goode family gone. Already the siblings were being blamed for bad luck. Stammerin' Eddie's coffee machine broke. It was an antique that made the best coffee in the state. Sophia Ward lost three front teeth a week before her big acting job in a local cereal commercial. And Leda Bourreau's soufflé fell, the first in the five years since she'd left chef school.

Whether Nolan believed the Goode witches being back had anything to do with these events didn't matter. The townspeople believed themselves to be cursed by their presence. The trick was going to be making them leave without letting them know he was making them leave.

Nolan put his truck into gear and drove up the overgrown drive to park in front of the house. The evening sun was beginning to set. He tilted the rearview mirror to check his hair and ran his hands through it a few times.

When he reached to open the door, a woman in a square-dancing dress walked from the house. Her bright red hair was pulled into a bun on the top of her head. She carried a garden gnome statue and placed it in the overgrown weed patch by the front porch.

"Nolan Dawson." The woman smiled and put her hands on her hips. "You have to be him. I would know the aura of the Dawson werewolves anywhere. I'm Polly."

Nolan stiffened and stopped midstride. He automatically glanced around.

Everyone in Lucky Valley knew the town was full of the supernatural, but no one talked about it out loud. His werewolf heritage was not something he told people about. His particular line found it impossible to control the wolf during a full moon, and he'd been chaining himself in the basement since puberty each time it passed over. His grandmother called it the Dawson curse. His grandfather blamed the Goode family.

His father didn't say anything as he'd broken his chains and was shot dead before he could attack a high school bus returning from a basketball game.

"I had a message to come by," Nolan said. "Do I need my inspection clipboard?"

"Oh, no, the house is fine," Polly dismissed with a wave. "You can pass it."

"That's not how it works, ma'am," Nolan said.

"Oh, sure it is. Now, come inside. I've been waiting for you."

Nolan frowned. *This* was the person who wrote him the note? He felt a little like a fool for trying too hard. He reached up and mussed his hair into its usual careless style and pulled his shirt from his jeans.

Nolan had already inspected the property and thought he knew what to expect, but when he walked inside, the house was in pristine condition—especially for being built in the 1800s. Tarnished doorknobs looked polished. Deteriorating wallpaper had been rehung, the brittle tears mended as if they had never existed. He breathed deeply, trying to smell a trace of the mildew and mold.

There was no non-magical way they could have done all the work that needed to be done.

This complicated things. If they could do this much in one night, there was no way citations would scare them off. He would have to take things to the next level... whatever that meant.

"See, fit as a fiddle, fine as a cat, hairy as a werewolf in the full moon." Polly winked at him. "No need to inspect."

"Masking an issue is not the same as fixing it. I have a job to do," Nolan said.

"Not tonight. Tonight, you're my special

guest." The woman winked again. "And I have plans for you."

Nolan wasn't sure how to answer. Was he... on a blind date... with Polly?

His friends' wives were always trying to set him up. How did he back out of this without hurting the woman's feelings?

He tilted his head to listen for movement. He focused his shifter hearing. At first there didn't seem to be anyone else in the home. Then with relief, he heard low voices coming from somewhere in the house.

"Whatever is in here won't change anything," Dante Goode's voice said from upstairs. Nolan stepped closer.

"Florus, I think things have already changed for us," Lily drawled. There was a wryness to her tone. "There is no going back. We can't ignore the present for the comfort of the familiar past. Now open that damned thing."

"You might want to retract those glowing eyes, or you'll give yourself away. They only now found out they're witches."

Polly's voice drew him from his eavesdropping. He realized he's started to shift in his effort to hear the conversation between the siblings. His nails had thickened and extended. The points of his teeth began to push his lips forward.

"They didn't know?" he asked in surprise as he calmed the beast within.

"People only know what they know." Polly gave a little skip as she tried to lead him toward the dining room. "And what they don't know, they rarely know they don't, like you."

"Like me?" Nolan didn't follow her as he continued to peer up the stairs. Gnomes were placed on the steps. He guessed that Lily must really like garden gnomes. She did have a lot of them around the property.

"Why, yes, I do like you," Polly said. "You're all squishy-squashy."

Nolan frowned. That wasn't a compliment. At least it didn't sound like one.

"Sugar bee, Florus," Polly called, "our dinner guest has arrived."

The siblings instantly stopped talking. Silence followed Polly's announcement. Nolan heard movement and a clicking sound.

Seconds later, a loud scream pierced the air.

Lily.

Nolan didn't think, just reacted. He darted up the stairs. The wolf inside him picked up her scent. He moved to go to the third floor. A large, furry creature jumped down the stairs and he dodged the animal, not sensing it to be a threat as he ran to face whatever was happening.

"What was that?" Lily demanded, breathless.

"I think it was a raccoon," Dante answered, sounding just as shaken. He crawled out of the small storage space at the top of the stairs. The door had been locked, so Nolan hadn't been able to inspect inside.

"It was the size of a tank." Lily appeared from one of the third-floor bedrooms, where she apparently had hidden. Her hair had been pulled back to the nape of her neck. Her eyes instantly found him and she gasped.

Nolan ducked his head, hoping she'd think his partial shift was a play of shadows across his face.

"Whatever was in the trunk, I think the monster raccoon ate it. But is it any surprise my inheritance is an empty old trunk with a giant hole chewed through the side so killer raccoons can jump out at me?" Dante stood, dusted his knees, and then followed his sister's gaze to Nolan.

"I heard a scream. Is everything all right?" he asked Lily. As confusion registered on her face, he realized she didn't know why he was there. He shifted awkwardly on his feet. "The raccoon is gone. He ran downstairs, more afraid of you than you are of him."

"Doubtful," Dante said. "He tried to attack my head."

Lily's eyes darted to her brother and then back to him. "Did you bring another novel?"

"Novel?" He didn't understand what she meant by that.

"Stack of citations," she clarified. "We haven't had time to get to everything yet."

"Ah, oh, um...?"

"I invited him to dinner," Polly yelled from below.

"We have nothing to eat in this place," Lily called back, "so I'm not sure how we're going to serve dinner."

"You worry more than you should," Polly scolded. She sounded closer than before and appeared at the bottom of the stairs moments later.

Nolan made a move to leave. There was no reason to stay where he wasn't wanted, and the entire situation had become uncomfortable.

"Oh, the food's coming." Polly pointed her finger toward the ceiling. "I'll get the door."

"We'll be down in a second, Polly," Lily said. "We just want to check this room first."

Nolan didn't hear anyone outside. "I'll be..." He let his words trail off into an incoherent mumble as he turned to follow Polly.

"There's nothing in there," Dante said, shutting the door before Lily could go back inside. He held his arm out to make Lily go down the stairs before him.

Nolan glanced between the siblings and then led the way down. When they reached the bottom level, he said, "You've done a lot of work on this place in a short time."

He'd meant it as a conversation starter but could see by the expressions on their faces they didn't take it as one. An uncomfortable silence filled the front hall. The more he tried not to look at Lily, the more he found himself glancing at her.

"It wasn't us," Dante said. "Polly took care of it."

"It looks nice." Nolan followed them into the dining room.

"Thank you." Lily paused close to him. "I'm sorry if I was rude. It's been a demanding day and I'm trying to keep it together but—"

Something splashed before she could finish. Nolan wasn't sure how he'd missed it, but there was a children's pool on the dining room table with a lobster inside.

"That's Herman," Dante said, "Polly's friend."

Lily covered her mouth and started to laugh.

She tried to speak, but the laughter only increased. She placed her hands on the back of a chair and leaned over.

"Lily?" Dante asked, apparently concerned by the behavior.

"Insane," Lily said, gasping for breath. "All of this is insane. There's a pet lobster on the table. Garden gnomes are taking over the yard. Our only relative is a crazy lady who thinks we're witches—and even crazier, I believe her." She gestured at Nolan. "This guy... I don't even know why he's here for a dinner party we didn't know we were having, in a house that should be falling down around our heads, from a mother who—"

Her words stopped abruptly, and she walked from the dining room toward the kitchen.

"Yeah, sorry about Lily. She'll be fine in a moment. She's under a lot of stress right now," Dante said. "She didn't mean any of that. Those citations and this house have her a little on edge."

"And our lawn is on fire," Lily called. "Of course. Why not?"

Nolan sprang into action. He rushed toward her. An orange glow lit her face from outside the window. She didn't appear to be in a hurry to stop it as she watched the flames. He darted toward the side entrance and tripped on a gnome on his way down the steps to the yard. The fire seemed contained on the lawn, but he wasn't sure how long that would last. He ran around the side of the house to where he kept a garden hose in his truck bed.

Polly paid a pizza delivery boy. Not many people would come to the Goode house. The kid looked glassy-eyed as he handed the box to the witch. Nolan didn't have time to wonder if the kid was under a spell as he grabbed the hose.

He sprinted to the side of the house and attached the hose before turning on the water and returning to the back. Lily stood inside the back door, watching the flames.

Nolan sprayed the fire, trying to hit its base. As the flames lessened, Dante joined his side and tried tamping a few down with his foot.

When they finished, Nolan dropped the hose and took several deep breaths. He tried to detect who might have started the fire, but the smell of smoke and accelerant masked any scent. Dusk was settling over the surrounding valley and forest. He focused his eyes on the nearby tree line, but anyone who had been there was long gone.

Realizing he was using his enhanced senses, he closed his eyes before the siblings saw the inner glow.

"Get out," Lily stated.

He glanced up at her in surprise. "What?"

She lifted her finger and traced cursive letters in the air as she pointed at the burnt grass. "Get out."

He went toward her and climbed the steps to join her in the doorway. Sure enough, the words "get out" were spelled on the law in scorched letters.

Dante gestured at the siding. "Someone's not very creative but they're getting their point across."

Nolan turned to see the same message spray-painted on the house. "That wasn't here last week when MacIver's office asked me to inspect the property for the trust."

"Who would do such a thing? We just arrived in Lucky Valley." Lily hugged her arms over her chest and shivered.

"The…" Nolan started to answer, compelled to ease her worry, but then stopped himself.

"What?" Lily studied him.

Since they both stood by the back door, she was closer than she'd ever been to him. The fragrance of flowers and a light perfume wafted over him. His body stiffened in response, and he moved down a step to put distance between them.

"I can tell you were about to say something. Do you know who did this?"

"The Goode family doesn't have the best reputation." Nolan wanted to be diplomatic in his response, but there was no pleasant way of telling someone they were a pariah because of their ancestry.

"What Marigold sin are we paying for now?" Dante muttered, not looking like he expected an answer.

"Everyone knows the Goode family is…" Nolan paused. None of this was his place to say. He was supposed to encourage them to leave, not make friends with them.

"Is…?" Dante prompted.

"Insane?" Lily suggested.

"Neglectful?" Dante added.

"Broken?" Lily arched a brow in his direction.

"Powerful." Nolan lowered his voice.

"Powerful?" Dante laughed. "Because of the trust money? Maybe once, but not anymore. There are only three Goodes left that we know about and, believe me, *powerful* is not a word I'd use to describe us."

Nolan knew there was no point in pretending he didn't know. "Not powerful as in politically influential, though I suppose that is part of it.

Powerful as in *powerful*. Magic. Witchcraft. Spells. Potions. Curses. The whole gamut."

"You too with the witches?" Dante kicked at the wet, scorched earth, disrupting it.

"Do you know what Lucky Valley is?" Nolan questioned.

"A town?" Dante said.

"An old ghost town that my family supposedly founded?" Lily didn't take her gaze off of him.

"A place to get pizza," Polly announced, appearing from the kitchen. She pulled Lily's arm. "Come, come, dinner's ready."

Lily stumbled back but continued to follow Polly as if she had no choice.

Dante started to move past him but then stopped. "She doesn't date."

"What?" Nolan turned his attention away from the women.

"Lily. She doesn't date." Dante slapped him on the shoulder. "Thought I'd save you the trouble of trying before you embarrassed yourself."

"I wasn't going to ask her out," Nolan denied.

"Whatever you say." Dante chuckled. "But I see how you look at her. I'm telling you, she won't be interested. Better men than you have tried."

Nolan wondered if Dante knew he sounded like a jerk, or if he really thought he was helpful with his warning. At the man's smirk, he guessed jerk.

Two could play that game.

"Let me save you some trouble. This town is full of supernatural creatures—and they blame your family for taking all of their good luck, amongst other transgressions." Nolan let his eyes flash with a shift. The man gasped as he brushed past. "I'm telling you, so you know that fire and spray paint are just the tip of the iceberg. Not everyone is happy you're here to claim your inheritance."

Chapter Six

"You know something, don't you?" Lily cornered Nolan in the living room. She had wanted to ask him that very question all through the awkward meal.

Polly had insisted they eat, despite the fact there had been someone setting fires on the lawn. The woman had ended up doing most of the talking during the meal to distract them. And, as much as Lily wanted to stand up and shout how ridiculous it was to eat after such an event, every time she tried, her legs felt shaky and she found herself reaching for another slice of pizza, as if shoving food into her mouth would plug the noise about to come out. The impulse didn't appear to be completely hers.

Why Polly had invited the man to the house

was beyond her. He wasn't inspecting anything, and he didn't look like he *wanted* to be there. Actually, he looked like he'd been forced at knife-point to sit at the table with them—a table that showcased a live lobster who stared at them while they ate.

Nolan had avoided Polly's questions by giving non-answers, and there was some kind of weird thing going on between Nolan and Dante. Her brother had practically glared in the man's direction.

When he didn't answer, she prompted, "Well?"

"I know a lot of things." It was like the man tried to be frustratingly obtuse on purpose. Each time Nolan spoke, his words seemed measured and purposefully enigmatic.

There were times in life when you met someone, and the conversation flowed naturally. She felt like that should have been the case with Nolan, but for some reason there was a block between them. He kept himself on guard.

"About the fire," Lily clarified.

For a brief moment, she had considered letting the flames have the house. Her emotions were torn when it came to the Goode Estate and Lucky Valley. Maybe it would be better if there was no house to move to. The urge to run away was strong.

"You were about to say something before Polly dragged me inside," Lily insisted. "Do you know who's threatening us?"

He looked as if he might lie to her, but then sighed. "Your family doesn't have the best reputation in town. People here are afraid of you. I wouldn't expect them to show up at your door with a welcome casserole anytime soon. So, no, I can't say who did it. I can say there are probably several people who could have done it."

Lily appreciated his frankness. "I'm not my ancestors. I don't know who they were or what they did."

"I believe you." He nodded. "But I'm not sure that will matter."

Lily sat on the couch. The firm cushion wasn't inviting, but she didn't care. She braced her elbows on her knees, leaned over and ran her fingers into her hair to hold her head. Her voice soft, she asked, "Have you ever been drained to the point of emotional exhaustion?"

He didn't answer. She didn't expect him to. It was an overshare of information.

Still, that didn't stop her from looking at him expectantly. "How do I fix it? Who do I need to win over in town? How do I find out who wants us gone enough to do these things? Are we in danger?"

Nolan stared at the empty fireplace next to the couch.

"Never mind. This isn't your problem. For all I know, you probably want us gone too. You did try to convince us to sell at the attorney's office." Lily leaned back. She looked at the fireplace that held his attention. She considered the light fixtures and old furniture. She tried to imagine living in the old house with Jesse and Dante.

Home. That is all they ever wanted.

Echoes from the past whispered along the edge of her consciousness. There were memories on the fringes of her thoughts, memories from childhood that she never thought about. She had never let the past stop her, so why should she start now?

Lily stood. "I'll contact you when we're ready for the next inspection. And we *will* be ready. You can let whoever know that we're not leaving Lucky Valley. I don't care if every contractor in a hundred-mile radius turns us down. This is our home now, and we're going to—"

"I'll help you."

The words were quiet, and she wasn't sure she'd heard him.

"I'm sorry, I didn't catch that."

His eyes met hers. "I said I'll help you. I know this town. For the most part, they're good people, but you won't know what you're getting yourself into if you go poking around. Things are not what they seem, and people like their secrets."

"Why would you help me?" What was his angle?

"You have to bring this property up to code, that's just the law, but in my past career I was a contractor. Actually, I worked almost every job on a construction site. I can get you up and running."

She stepped closer, studying his face. "Why would you do all this?"

"Because the trust would pay me, and I need the work." His arms lifted over his chest as if that would keep her from coming closer. "I know you might find it a conflict of interest, the code inspector also working to fix the codes, but I give you my word that I'm fair. If at any time you find it otherwise, you can fire me and refuse to pay."

"I still don't understand why you would do this." Lily felt there was more to him, and she wanted to peel back the layers to see what he was hiding. "It won't make you very popular in town if we're as unliked as you say."

"I wouldn't say unliked, as much as feared."

Instinct told her she could trust him. Logic told her to be wary. Which did she listen to?

"Where did you two run off to?" Polly called.

Lily grabbed Nolan's arm and pulled him toward the front stairs. She tried to walk softly so Polly wouldn't be able to find them. She gestured that he should stay quiet and follow her.

Lily tiptoed as fast as she could, but a stair creaked. She bit her lip, freezing to see if Polly had heard.

"There you are," Polly exclaimed from below.

"Nolan has agreed to work for the trust." Lily motioned to the top of the stairs. Saying, *he agreed to work for me*, seemed too strange. "We're going to make a list of where I'd like him to start."

"Not as interesting as a rendezvous, but I think it's an excellent idea. I like a man around the house." Polly grinned.

"Hey, what about me?" Dante asked, his voice pouty.

"Someday, you'll be a man, Florus." Polly disappeared from the bottom of the stairs and Lily continued up. "Don't be in too big of a hurry to grow up."

"I'm twenty-six," Dante stated.

"Yes, and such a big boy you are, too."

Lily couldn't help the small laugh. Hearing a

sound, she glanced back to see Nolan trying to suppress his amusement.

Lily moved to the master bedroom on the second floor so they could talk privately. A giant wardrobe sat against the far wall. The dark wood had been carved to depict mythological woodland creatures along the top and mermaids swimming around the bottom. It matched the thick paneled sides of the bed frame.

"Your aunt is a character," Nolan said. "She must have been fun to be around as a child."

"I wouldn't know. The first time I talked to her was like a month ago when she called me to say I needed to come to Colorado to claim my inheritance. I almost hung up on her for being a phishing scam, but she knew enough information about my mother to make her sound credible."

Nolan glanced around the room. "You want me to start in your bedroom?"

Lily looked at the made bed. "Oh, I guess. I didn't really think about which room would be mine."

He pointed behind her. "I'm assuming that bright blue luggage is a little too girly for your brother, and not girly enough for Polly."

He was right.

"I don't care where you start. Just get rid of that stack of citations you gave me," she dismissed. "What do you mean, feared? What did my relatives do?" Running footsteps sounded overhead. Lily looked up at the ceiling. "What is that?"

"Every old house makes its own noises," Nolan dismissed. "You'll get used to it."

"You don't think it's another animal, do you?"

"No." He seemed fairly confident, so she let it drop. "To answer your question, Lucky Valley was founded by the Goodes and the Crawfords during the 1800s as a refuge for certain types of people who weren't wanted in the old country. Jedediah Crawford had struck gold, and the Goode family had the money to set up a full mining operation. They combined forces and together they built this town."

"Go on," she prompted when he paused. Getting conversation out of him was like trying to get a straight answer out of Polly—darn near impossible.

"All I know are the stories I heard as a kid." The light through the window had dimmed, and he reached to flip on a light switch. The lights flickered. "I'll fix that."

"The stories you heard as a kid..." she reminded him. There was no way she was letting him go until she heard why someone wanted to burn the lawn and spray paint the house.

"Some say the Goodes became greedy. Some say the Crawfords became careless. Others claim it was a pact with the devil. And a few think maybe it was the very first of the bad luck curse. The one thing everyone agrees on is that the Goodes and the Crawfords did not get along, and it was that feud that began the run of bad luck the town became known for." Nolan walked to the window and looked out. His shoulders lifted as if he took a deep breath. "Out there, in Unlucky Valley—that's what locals call the remains of the first town—there were a series of calamitous events. In the span of three days, a church went up in flames, a disease spread out over the crops, and the mine caved in."

"And they think my ancestors did this?"

"They think it was a byproduct of the magic being used between the feuding families. Everyone in town had a family member who died that day, most had more than one. The two families couldn't agree on a way to save the miners and refused to work together. Their individual efforts weren't enough, and by the time they'd dug through to where the men were holed up, a hundred and eighteen workers died."

"That's tragic. So did my ancestors sabotage the mines? Or skip corners with safety?"

"They say it was magic."

"So they magically dried up crops, destroyed churches, and ruined their money making gold mines? That makes little sense. Why would they do that? It doesn't seem like it was beneficial for anyone." Lily shook her head. "Maybe it was nothing more than plain old bad luck."

He stiffened. "I wouldn't dismiss the stories in front of others, if I were you."

"I didn't mean to insult anyone, but I'm still trying to determine how a mining accident—in a time where there were probably hundreds of unsafe mining accidents in this country—equals my siblings and me being evil."

"Well, your mother…"

Lily sighed and nodded her head. "Right. Never mind. Now it makes sense."

Marigold wouldn't have helped the family reputation.

"I don't want to speak ill of the dead," he said.

"The last time I saw my mother, she was standing outside my apartment window, tapping her fingernails on the glass while muttering nonsense. She was too thin. Her hair looked like wild birds might have been living in it, and her black lace dress was in tatters. When I tried to go outside to get her help, she'd vanished. All that was left was a strange symbol drawn in blood on the glass. So please, don't feel the need to sugar-coat anything on my behalf."

"They say she stirred dark magic when she married a Goode and awoke the old curse. Like I said, I was a kid at the time, but I remember people shunning her in the streets. We were all scared of her. Bad things were happening, and every misstep was blamed on your family. I remember her how you described—thin, almost skeletal, with overgrown hair and nails. She always talked even though no one was there to answer her. We were told to stay away from Marigold Crawford Goode, or she'd steal our souls and leave us wandering."

"I don't know about soul stealing." Lily surprised herself at the small defense.

He again turned his attention toward the window. "You didn't ask me why the people who came here needed a refuge."

"Wasn't it because of religious persecution, or people being exiled, or potato famines, or something? My history is a little rusty, but I'm pretty sure that's why most people came to America in the first place."

"That's true, but the one thing that joined

everyone in Lucky Valley, the one thing that still joins us is," Nolan turned, his eyes glowing with the inner light of a shift, "we're all supernaturals."

"Supernat…" Her words trailed off as she stared at him. At first she tried to tell herself it was a trick of the overhead light on his face, but as he stepped closer, the yellow glow didn't leave. "So you're a witch too?"

"No, only the Goodes and Crawfords are witches. The Dawsons are werewolves, shapeshifters. No matter who we marry, that always seems to come out as the most dominant gene, at least in the males."

"Are you…?" She reached her hand out, compelled to touch him. "Are you going to shift now?"

"No."

"But…" How cool would it have been to see a real live werewolf? Then again, maybe not. That usually didn't end well in movies. She wasn't sure if she should feel disappointed or completely freaked out. Maybe she was broken. All of Polly's crazy had done something to her mentally.

"I'm not a circus act."

"You brought it up, not me." Lily crossed her

arms over her chest. "I think it was a fair question, considering you went all crazy eyes on me."

The glow went away. "I don't have crazy eyes."

"Um, yeah you do." She nodded several times.

"I do not. They shift to improve my vision."

Lily sighed. "I guess all I have to do is prove to the town that I'm not my mother, and that I'm not going to open an unsafe mining operation anytime soon. Shouldn't be too hard."

"I have shifter eyes." He hadn't let her comment go.

"Fine. You have shifter eyes."

"Thank you." The lights flashed overhead, and he studied the light fixture. "What are you going to do?"

"I don't know. Maybe I'll turn this into a bed and breakfast. There's so much room, and I've worked in customer service for years. I could hire a few people to help out. I need to earn money for what isn't covered by the trust fund. A girl's gotta eat." Lily didn't know what compelled her to say such a thing, but the moment it was past her lips, a bed and breakfast felt like an actual business plan. She wasn't sure about having people staying in her home, but this didn't feel like her home. Maybe she could live in one the cottages, away from the guests.

"The bathrooms will need to be updated."

Lily chuckled. "That's it? No, you can't do it? No, the town will never let that happen?"

"You'll need a bigger water tank. Individual heaters. It can get warm in the summer months, so I'd recommend individual air conditioning units in the rooms, as well. As to the rest, your sanity remains to be seen, and tourism is good for local economies."

"Even if it's tainted Goode-Crawford tourism?"

"Lily, I won't lie to you." He touched her arm. Warmth spread from his fingers, causing her to shiver. She couldn't pull her gaze from him, watching for signs of a physical change. "Supernatural threats are not like human ones. This won't be easy. You won't know how much danger you're in until you figure out who is threatening you. If it's a couple of kids daring each other to taunt the witch, you're fine."

"You don't think it's kids, do you?" She continued to study his expression, trying to decipher what he was not telling her.

"There is no way to explain to you the people who call Lucky Valley home. Hollywood movies only touch upon a small percentage of what's real, and they often get it wrong."

"I'm a witch without magic witch-powers. I'm a Goode *and* a Crawford who doesn't know a single thing about her families. What I don't know could probably fill a dozen spell books, but the one thing I am is a fighter. I'm not afraid. I'm not going to quit. I'll solve any mystery that is put in front of me. So, mystery of the lawn-burning, spray-painting bandits is priority number one. Then the mystery of my missing witch powers if I even have them. And finally, the mystery of the creaky noises, leaking basement appliances, and the hopefully disappearing stack of citations will be last."

Nolan's fingers tightened briefly and then released their hold. "I believe you. It's a good thing you hired me."

As he tried to leave, she touched his arm to stop him. "Why a good thing?"

"You're clearly determined. I think it's going to get you in trouble, especially in this town." A small smile curled the side of his lips. "You're going to need protection, even if you don't realize it yet."

At that, she laughed. She was hardly a damsel in distress. "And what makes you think you can protect me?"

His eyes flashed with gold as he stepped back-ward toward the door. He pointed at his chest and said, "Werewolf."

The parting move would have been confident if not for the fact he tripped on a gnome placed near the door. She hadn't noticed the statue until he was stumbling out of the room into the hall.

Lily waited until she heard him right himself. "Gee, I feel so much safer already."

"You should," he said, not coming back into the room. "I'm really good at what I do."

Chapter Seven

Lily had made a grave mistake. It wasn't that she had gone to Stammerin' Eddies to drink the best-worst coffee in town, or that she had tried to patronize local businesses to prove she cared about the new town she was moving into. It wasn't even that she had tried to talk to a total of seven locals, the last of whom had grabbed her child and ran.

The woman actually ran down Main Street.

Down freaking Main Street.

Compared to this, those things were nothing.

Compared to this, well... nothing compared to this.

Lily looked down the tree to where the cat-human and the dog-human circled beneath her. If the strange noises in her new house, the randomly appearing gnomes, and glowing eyes of her contractor-handyman hadn't convinced her that Lucky Valley was full of the unexplained, this definitely did the trick. The cat roared and hissed. The dog growled and barked. They both looked like they wanted to eat her.

Lily tried to catch her breath as she hugged the trunk and balanced on a tree branch. Her hand shook as she fumbled for the phone inside her pocket. It slipped from her fingers and she caught it between her legs. Beneath her, the shifters continued to pace and stare up at her. The cat roared louder and jumped several feet off the ground. She jerked out of his way so he couldn't grab her.

"Breathe, Lily, breathe," she whispered.

She brought up her phone contacts and tapped Nolan's name. The dog jumped, and then the cat, as if competing to see who could get closer. She yelped in fright as claws knocked off her shoe.

"This is Nolan," he answered.

"Where are you?" she demanded.

"Lily? Is that you?"

"Where are you?"

"Near the woods outside of town. Why? Is everything all right?"

"Nolan, you know how you said I would need

you, and that I was lucky to have you because you knew the supernatural stuff around here and—"

"Whoa, easy, calm—"

"—I didn't know about that stuff and—"

"Slow down."

"—there is a cat and dog trying to eat me and I don't particularly want to be on the menu—"

"Wait, what are you talking about? You're not making any sense. Can you get to better reception?"

"No, I can't get to better reception," she yelled. "I'm stuck in a tree."

"A tree?"

"Seriously, is this the best help you're going to —*ah*!" Lily felt a tug on her shoe and the second one fell off. "I think I found who has been threatening us. And they want me dead."

"Lily, where are you?" Nolan's voice filled with concern, though she would have liked a little more urgency in his tone to indicate he understood the full horror of her situation.

"Some park with a statue of a naked mermaid." She lost her balance for a moment and wobbled on the branch.

"Poseidon Park. I'm on my way. Who's after you?" Nolan asked.

"A cat and a dog," she said.

"Wait, what? Seriously?"

"Dog-man and cat-man," she said. "I don't know what to call them. One second they're smoking by the public restrooms and the next they're sprouting fur and chasing me up a tree."

"Catshifter, wolfshifter?" he asked.

"Are you really going to lecture me about my language choices?" she demanded. "Never mind. Some bodyguard contractor you are. I should have called the police."

"No, wait. Here's what I need you to do. Tell them you're on the phone with Nancy Felinus."

"I don't think they're going to care, Nolan."

"Just do it, Lily." He mimicked her tone.

"I'm on the phone with Nancy Felinus," she yelled.

The cat stopped jumping and grabbed the dog's arm.

"Now say she's calling Darcy," Nolan said.

"And she's going to call Darcy," Lily yelled before ad-libbing, "She's not pleased."

To her surprise, it worked. The two shifters ran off, leaving her in the tree.

"Nolan, I can't believe that worked. Who are Nancy and Darcy? Local law? Animal patrol?"

"Their mothers," he said with a small laugh.

"Trust me, that's worse than anything law enforcement would do."

The catshifter came running back, and Lily stiffened. She drew the phone back, readying to pelt him with it.

He held his hands up as the fur retracted into his face. He looked like a high schooler. "Please don't tell her you caught us smoking, Ms. Goode. We're sorry for scaring you. We were just joking around. I promise, we won't do it again."

Lily frowned. He even sounded like a kid. His young voice held more fear than threat in his human form. "And you'll stop vandalizing my property?"

"I don't know what that means, ma'am. We don't go on Goode land." He bounced on his feet as if he might run away at any second. "I swear. We know better than to tempt the spirit of Marigold Crawford Goode."

"Lily? Lily?"

She realized Nolan was still on the phone yelling at her.

"Good point. You think your mom is frightening, you better get home before *my* mother comes," Lily told the kid, feeling only mildly guilty using Marigold as a threat. He nodded and ran. She lifted the phone. "Yeah, I'm here. All good. Thanks."

Embarrassment set in as she realized she had treed herself for a couple of prankster teenagers.

"I'm near the park," he said.

"No, it's fine. I'm fine. I'm…" Lily grimaced. Adrenaline had helped her up the tree. She wasn't exactly sure how she was going to get out of it. "I'm stuck."

Nolan laughed. "What do you see? I'll come find you."

"No, it's fine." She adjusted on the branch. "I'll figure it out. Sorry to bother—"

She lost her balance, and the phone fell.

"—you," she finished, even though the phone bounced on the ground beneath her. "Crap."

Lily looked around the park. The playground and jogging path were empty. The teenagers had pulled off her shoes, so she didn't have anything to protect her feet as she tried to wrap her legs around the trunk and ungracefully slide her way down. The bark scraped her hands and arms and poked through her socks to scratch her arches.

"Ow, ow, dammit, ow," she swore as she tried to shimmy her way down.

A loud thump and crash of leaves sounded overhead, and she lost her grip.

Lily landed on top of her cellphone and a shoe. The wind was knocked from her lungs as she lay on her back. The sound had been made by a squirrel jumping branches. It paused to look down at her and chittered as if laughing.

When she could move, she rolled onto her side, off the shoe. She coughed, reaching behind her to slide the phone from beneath her butt. Her hands throbbed, her back ached, but at least no one had witnessed what happened and she had her pride intact.

"Are you all right, Lily? That looked like a nasty fall." Nolan's feet appeared close to her head.

Nope. She was wrong. Her pride was nowhere to be seen.

"Why didn't you wait for me?" He knelt beside her and then looked up into the tree branches.

"I don't know why everyone in town is so scared of me. Apparently, the only one I'm a danger to is myself." Lily tried to push up, but it hurt too badly.

"You're bleeding," he said. "I don't think you should move."

"I'm fine. Just winded." She let him help her to her feet, mainly because he didn't give her much of a choice.

"You keep saying that, but you don't look fine," Nolan said.

"Um, thanks?" she mumbled sarcastically.

Lily assumed being upright would somehow make her feel better. Why she thought that, she had no clue. More body parts began to throb in pain. Her left knee and ankle refused to bear weight. Her backside felt bruised, and her tailbone broken. She turned her arms to see angry red scrapes along her flesh.

Nolan tried to lift her into his arms so he could carry her. She swatted the back of her wrist at him. "What are you doing?"

"You need a doctor."

"I can wal—"

"Oh my god, woman, seriously? You are the most hardheaded person I've ever met." Nolan crossed his arms over his chest. "Okay. Walk. Let's see it."

Lily wanted to prove she could, that she didn't need his or anyone's help. She had always prided herself on being independent and strong. A girl had to grow up like that when she didn't have someone around to offer guidance.

She tried to take a step and tears filled her eyes. She managed two limps before she had to stop. Her voice was quiet as she whispered, "I can't."

"I didn't catch that."

"Nolan, will you please assist me to the car?"

She tried turning her head to look at him, but her neck hurt too.

"Yes." The word held no mocking as he slipped an arm around her back and lifted her against his chest. He carried her toward where he'd parked his pickup at an awkward angle. The driver's side was parallel to the curb and the back tire had driven up onto the grass. "Where is your car?"

"Downtown. I wanted to walk and explore." She grunted as he stepped off a curb. "Oh, my phone. I need my phone. And my shoes. I only have the one pair of sneakers."

He lowered her feet slowly to the ground and then helped her onto the bench seat. She leaned to the side, unable to get comfortable. It was only a few seconds, but Nolan appeared by the driver side door holding her shoes and phone. She glanced back toward the tree, surprised by the speed with which he had run there and back.

"I'll try to take it easy on any potholes, but I'm getting you to the hospital." Nolan put the truck into gear and slowly drove off the grass onto the road. Lily watched his face. The vehicle bounced, and he flinched for her. "Sorry."

"Can you drive me home?" she asked. "And then maybe bring my brother downtown so he can pick up the car?"

"Hospital."

"But—"

"Hos-pi-tal," he enunciated.

"You're…" She wrinkled her nose. "Difficult."

"So are you." His smile was strained.

She realized he was concerned. It was strange to think someone who was not one of her siblings was worried about her. He sped up, taking a corner. She watched his hands, bracing herself every time the wheel began to turn.

"I was wrong about the kids. They aren't the ones vandalizing the house," Lily said. "The kid seemed genuinely scared when I asked him about going on Goode land."

"What are you talking about?"

"On the phone, I told you I knew who was threatening us. I was wrong."

"I could have told you that. Luke and Patrick are troublemakers, but they're not stupid."

"The wolf kid…?"

"Luke."

"Is he family?"

"Because all wolfshifters are related?" He gave a small laugh.

"I don't know." She closed her eyes and tried to turn away from him. The new angle hurt too badly, and again, she was forced to face him.

"No. Not all shifters are related. Luke is from a different line. He's a decent kid, but his family is a little rowdy, even for us animals."

Lily liked the sound of his voice. He distracted her from the pain. She stared at his hands on the wheel until her vision blurred. "Keep talking."

"Lily? Lily, look at me. Open your eyes. Say something. Lily!"

"Keep talk…"

Chapter Eight

Nolan cursed as he sped toward the hospital. When she'd called him, he'd just finished running the length of the woods surrounding her Victorian. There were a few suspicious tracks, but nothing he could prove was a threat. For all he knew, they could have been made by hikers on a nature walk.

He'd actually thought it was a city council member calling—*yet again*—to get an update on his progress. Nolan didn't want to tell them he had changed his mind about chasing Lily away. If he did, they'd task someone else with the job— if they hadn't already. The paint and fire were clearly meant to scare the siblings.

The truck hit a small pothole. He held Lily

steady as she slumped over. Her head dropped to the seat.

"Lily, answer me," he demanded. She didn't move. He drove faster. His shifter hearing focused on her chest and he listened to her raspy breathing. "Just hold on. We're almost there."

Nolan saw the hospital in the distance and turned to drive into the parking lot. Only, the truck didn't turn. He gripped the wheel, circling it to go left. Instead, it went straight. He slammed on the brakes, but they didn't work. The wheel jerked against his fingers and he let go. The truck drove itself away from the hospital.

"Lily, are you doing this?"

She didn't answer.

Nolan sat her up on the seat and brushed the hair out of her face. The truck slowed as it came to a stop sign. "Hold on. We're getting out of here."

Nolan slid her next to him and opened the door. When the truck stopped on its own, he hopped out. He turned to pull her into his arms, intent on running her to the hospital. However, the truck door struck his arm and sent him stumbling before it slammed shut. The truck took off down the road without him, increasing speed.

"Lily," Nolan yelled. A shift rippled over his body. Bones popped as fur covered flesh. He leapt after the truck. His werewolf form didn't turn him into a four-legged animal, but it gave him a strength his human form did not possess. He could run faster and longer, leap higher, heal faster. But he wasn't Superman. He could be injured or killed. And he couldn't outrun a speeding truck.

Nolan sprinted, trying to catch his runaway pickup. The vehicle took a corner a little too fast, and the tires skid on loose gravel. The delay it caused was enough to allow him to jump on the bumper and hold the tailgate. His claws dug into the black plastic bed liner. The truck turned again, throwing his feet out from under him. He held on, using all the strength he had to pull himself up and over the back.

Breathing hard, he went to the window to look in at Lily. She lay unconscious on the seat, sliding and bouncing with the vehicle's movement. The back window had a slider that opened, but it was latched on the inside. Nolan knocked on the glass. He'd break it if he wasn't worried about the shards landing on her.

"Lily, I need you to wake up." His voice was gruff in his shifted form.

Nolan stood, looking over the cab. The truck took them out of town toward Lily's home, which also happened to be in the direction of the old mines. If someone was causing this to happen, it would be a sick poetic justice to magically crash a Goode-Crawford descendent into the place where so many had died.

A fear worked over him, and he had to wonder if this wasn't just meant to scare Lily, but to kill her.

He knocked harder, leaning back down to yell, "Lily!"

Small puffs of white left her lips.

Nolan went to the driver's side and reached for the handle. They passed the driveway to Lily's house. It was as he feared. They were on their way to the old mines. He held on, ready to heave himself around to the front seat. He opened the door, careful to make sure Lily didn't start to slide out.

The door slammed shut a little too forcefully.

"Dammit!" He jammed a claw into the seam of the slider window to break the latch. It took a couple of sweeps and he chipped his claw, but he finally managed to get the window open.

Nolan reached down to touch Lily. She was cool but breathing. "I don't know who you are, but you need to get your spectral ass out of my truck!"

The wheel turned. Nolan swept his arm back

and forth over the driver's seat. Air as cold as a winter's day met his hand.

"I'm warning you. You're haunting the wrong pickup."

The faint sound of a cackle answered him.

"Who summoned you? What do you want? If you hurt her, I swear I'll exorcise—"

"*Yee-haw!*" came the disembodied answer.

The truck turned a hard right, kicking up dirt. Nolan had to hold on to the window frame to keep from flying out of the back. His feet slid down the truck bed and his hip hit the hard liner. He jerked back and forth several times and braced himself for impact.

To his surprise, the truck came to a stop.

Nolan pulled himself up. They had circled around to Lily's house. Deep ruts tore up her yard from where the truck had off-roaded its way to the porch. He didn't stop to consider why as he jumped out and flung open the passenger door. There wasn't much room between him and the railing and he stood in the overgrown flower bed. He pulled Lily from the pickup and held her against him.

"Dante! Polly! We need help," he shouted.

The passenger door slammed shut. His truck began to move as Nolan cradled Lily against him. The vehicle took off toward the mines, skidding and sliding its back tires against the ground like it was driven by a teenage boy trying to impress his friends.

Nolan turned and tripped. He almost dropped her but managed to pull her tight against his chest. Lily bounced in his arms and moaned lightly. He glanced down, seeing an overturned gnome with a chipped face.

"What did you do to my—*Oh, wow, you're really hairy*." Dante appeared at the front door.

Polly was right behind Lily's brother. "Oh no. I was hoping the bad luck wouldn't affect her too, but it looks like with her missing powers, she's as susceptible to the curse as everyone else in town. And it's progressed fast. My potion is only half boiled. I can't counteract this fully yet."

"What happened?" Dante's question was less accusatory than before and more worried.

"She fell from a tree. I tried to take her to the hospital but…" He looked to the dust cloud where his truck disappeared. "I lost control of my vehicle."

"You wrecked—" Dante started to say.

"Quiet, Florus," Polly scolded. "Hold the door for Nolan."

"My name is—never mind. I'm calling an ambulance." Dante pulled a phone out of his pocket.

Polly flipped her hand toward Dante. The phone flew from his fingers onto the ground by his feet. "She'll be fine once we get her in the house. Her bad luck would increase at the hospital. Here, she'll be surrounded by a blanket of magical love."

"She needs a doctor," Nolan said. "Dante?"

"Yeah." Dante grabbed his phone off the ground before he opened the door to let Nolan past. He heard Lily's brother dialing for help.

Nolan laid Lily on the couch. Before he could speak, an object flew past his head. He turned to see who had thrown something at him, only to find Polly lowering her fingers and Dante holding an empty hand up to his ear.

"She needs a doctor, you crazy old bat, not a fairytale magic house," Dante said.

"Mind your manners. You're not too old to send to your room without supper, little boy," Polly answered, though her tone had no malice in it. "Now knock on wood. Stop borrowing trouble. Don't bring bad luck down on this house."

"Who needs a doctor?"

Nolan looked down at the weak question. Lily's eyes had opened, and she blinked slowly. He stroked the hair back from her face. "You do. You were in an accident. You fell. Where does it hurt?"

"It tingles," she mumbled.

"I've got something that might help." Polly ran from the room.

Dante picked up his broken phone. "Lily, I need your phone."

"It's in my truck, broken," Nolan answered for her. He started to look for his when Lily grabbed his wrist.

"Dirty," she said.

"Dirty?" He glanced over her.

"Cowboy. Driving." Her grip tightened. "I saw him. I didn't see him, but I saw him. He kept laughing, a loud cackling sound."

"I think the truck was possessed," Nolan explained.

"Did you fall down too?" Dante asked. "You're both talking nonsense."

"Stan," Polly stated. She returned holding out a clear vial with pink liquid swirling with yellow. "Your presence here woke up Stan. That's unfortunate. That spirit is a handful. More bad luck."

"Of course ghosts are a thing," Dante mumbled. "Why wouldn't truck stealing ghosts be a real thing?"

Lily closed her eyes with a small moan.

"Wake up, dear, I need you to drink this for me." Polly knelt beside Nolan and held out the vial. She pinched it between her thumb and forefinger and shook it. "It's half done, and will half work, but it should spread out the bad luck so that it's in smaller doses." Polly pulled a cork off the top.

"I don't—" Lily tried to protest.

Polly poured the vial into her open mouth.

Lily sputtered and flailed her hands, too late to stop it. Little pink droplets dotted her cheek and chin only to be absorbed.

"There you go," Polly soothed. "I'm sorry we had to do it that way, but you were about to *bip* when I needed you to *bop*."

"Stop making up words," Lily groaned. Her color began to return to normal, and she took a deep breath. Her eyes appeared to focus better than before, and she tried to push up from the couch.

Nolan stood, to move out of her way.

"What did you give me? I feel strange—" The words barely made it past her lips when a loud creak sounded. Lily's eyes widened as the couch she sat on suddenly broke. The legs splinted to the side, and she dropped with the antique couch to the floor, protected by the cushioned seat.

"There you go, right as a turnip." Polly patted her shoulder. "Don't worry. You won't be unlucky forever, but just in case, maybe we should put your mattress on the floor and let you get some rest. Boys, help me carry her. That potion is going to make her sleep for a good long while."

Chapter Nine

Lily stared up at the ceiling where the chandelier light fixture used to be. Thankfully, no one had been under it when it came crashing down. Herman's pool had been moved to Polly's room and tiny shards of crystals littered the table and floor.

"What the hell was that?" Nolan appeared from the living room.

Lily pointed at the ceiling, not feeling the need to answer the obvious.

It was early in the morning, and he appeared buttoning his jeans as if he'd been sleeping and had just tugged them on. His feet were bare, and he stopped short of the glass. Scars puckered his chest and stomach. It looked like he'd been attacked by a... well, probably by a werewolf. It was unnerving, and she made a conscious effort not to look at him.

"What are you doing here? I would have thought you went home." Lily glanced toward the stairs, wondering why her brother and Polly weren't rushing down to investigate.

"Couldn't leave. Ghost stole my truck." He eyed the mess on the floor. "Careful of the glass. You're not wearing shoes."

Lily glanced at her feet and curled her naked toes. "Neither are you."

He walked around to the living room and appeared in the kitchen doorway, across the dining room from her.

Nolan held up a broom. "I'll clean this up. You should get some sleep."

A loud crash stopped her from answering. She inhaled sharply, jumping a little. A piece of broken crystal cut into her foot, and she retracted it from the floor as she hopped away from the mess. "Ow, ow, ow…"

"What happened?" Nolan asked.

"I stepped on a shard. It's not bad."

"What fell?"

"I don't know." Lily looked around finding another shattered light fixture, only this time it had landed at the bottom of the stairs. Broken glass trapped her in the hall. A gnome with a chipped face stood by the front door as if watching her. Polly's little statue friends were beginning to creep her out. "Wait, I see it. A light fixture fell in the front hall." She inched forward and looked up. Wires hung from the ceiling where the light fixture was supposed to be. "What's going on? It's like they've been ripped off the ceiling."

"I have no clue. I inspected all the fixtures and they were solid." The sound of the broom swished over his words. "Let me get this glass cleaned up and I'll check the others."

Suddenly, loud thumps and bangs sounded upstairs.

"Dante?" Lily yelled, considering how to get over the glass to the stairs. "Dante!"

"What the hell, Lily? Are you moving furniture in the middle of the night?" her brother answered.

"That's not me. I'm trapped downstairs."

Nolan appeared beside her with the broom. He swept a path toward the stairs for them. Lily tried to push past him, but he blocked her path and held out an arm to keep her between his back and the wall. "Stay behind me."

Lily frowned and pushed his arm out of her way so she could look upstairs. Footsteps ran overhead. A sleepy Dante appeared at the top of the stairs, but the running continued. The sound wasn't her brother.

"You have to say something to Polly about all these damned gnomes," Dante said. "She keeps putting them outside my bedroom like a—*whoa*."

"Who's running?" Lily asked. "Who else is up there?"

"Why do you keep thinking people are running?" Dante tilted his head. "I don't hear anything."

"Do you hear it?" she asked Nolan. He shook his head in denial. "I'm not crazy. There is someone running around this house."

"If you say there is, then there is. A ghost carjacked me, so who am I to judge what makes sense." Nolan's eyes flashed with an inner light.

"Where is Polly?" Lily hurried up the stairs.

"Dancing in the moonlight with Herman." Dante sighed. "I wouldn't go out there though. She said something about communing naked with the stars for answers to life's great mysteries."

Garden gnomes filled the upstairs hall, arranged in perfect lines like an army waiting to march. She stepped through them as she followed the sound of footsteps to the third story. "Hello? Who's up there?"

"Lily, stop, let me—"

"Stop acting like my boyfriend, Nolan," Lily interrupted. "I'm fine."

Dante snickered.

"I don't think I'm your boyfriend. But if someone dangerous is up there, I'm better equipped to handle it," Nolan answered.

"We'll both go," Lily said. For as brave as she tried to be, she was still frightened of the unknown that appeared to be lurking in her house. What if it was another ghost? Or a demon? Or an evil witch? Before coming to Colorado, she would never have believed there were such things as those, or as werewolves and catshifters. Now, she'd been treed by two and rescued by one. Nothing made rational sense.

"Oh, hey," Dante whispered. "Jesse called earlier when you were out."

"Is she coming?" Lily paused halfway up.

"Not so much. She said she wants nothing to do with our mother or her stupid safe deposit box, that we should burn the house down and any bad juju with it and come home." Dante didn't follow them up the stairs. "I'm inclined to agree with her."

"Do you still hear the running?" Nolan asked, interrupting their family talk.

Lily nodded and began leading the rest of the way up. She peaked through the balusters to the third floor. The sounds continued, followed by soft laughter.

"Maybe it's the creepy gnomes," Dante called.

"Stop trying to freak me out. Statues can't walk," Lily answered.

"Tell that to the gnome peeking down at you."

Lily automatically looked up. Nothing was there. "Shut up, Dante."

Several thumps sounded from within one of the bedrooms.

"Okay, *that* noise I heard," Nolan whispered.

Lily forced herself to be calm. She was glad Nolan had insisted on coming with her.

Thump.

Her hands trembled as she gripped the railing. Nolan briefly placed his hand over hers as if to steady her. They crept toward the bedroom.

Thump. Thump. Rattle. Thump.

Lily and Nolan reached for the door at the same time and pushed it with the tips of their fingers. The wood creaked as it opened.

Crreeaak. Thump. Bang.

They tilted their heads to look in.

"Damn, blasted. I…"

The sound was faint, but Lily heard the muffled words as if they came from underwater.

"Where'd ya go ya wee varmint…"

"Who's there?" Lily demanded.

Lily leaned closer to Nolan and tried not to make a sound as she stared at the room. A bed was in the middle next to a small dresser with a white porcelain bowl. The dresser slid an inch to the right and the foot of the bed lifted off the floor before thumping down.

Nolan again tried to push her behind him, but she resisted and moved to see who was causing all the noise. The bed bounced in a steady rhythm. She slowly leaned to the side to peek along the hidden edge of the bed.

The sound stopped. A gnome stood facing the corner like a punished child. Another gnome lay on the floor.

"I think Dante is right. It's the creepy gnomes." Lily stared at the little statues, watching for movement. A chill worked its way up her spine.

Nolan placed a hand on her arm. She jumped a little in surprise at the contact. He inhaled through his nose, and whispered, "Ghost." The word came out on a white puff of breath.

The bed lifted higher than before and crashed down.

When Lily turned her attention back to the

gnomes, they had not moved, but there was a pair of transparent legs sticking out from under the bed. The ghost's stained pants were frayed at the bottom hem and his boots were caked in dirt —if that was even possible.

"Uh, this house is not yours," Lily said. "Go to the light. Be gone, spirit."

"What are you doing?" Nolan whispered.

"Banishing him?" Lily shrugged. How the heck was she supposed to know what to do?

"How do you know it's a him?"

She pointed at the floor. "I assumed from the pants and boots, but I guess it could be a girl."

"All I see is a couple of gnomes."

The ghost's feet kicked, and the bed lifted up only to fall with a bang.

"Stop that!" she ordered.

The ghost cackled and wheezed and did it again. This time, he shimmied until his feet disappeared under the bed. All noises stopped.

"Is he gone?"

"Maybe?" She shrugged helplessly.

"Do you see him?"

Lily turned to Nolan and grabbed his upper arm. "Nolan, if I was really in a hospital with something in my brain making me hallucinate, you'd tell me, right? I mean, you'd tell me if I was insane or none of this was real, right?"

"Uh, Lily—"

"I'd be all right with that. Because if you expect me to bend over to look under the bed to see if there are any big-bad scaries lurking beneath there, I'm telling you now that I don't think I'm brave enough. I've seen how this horror movie ends. I'm not about to get sucked into a dark vortex by Cackles the Cowboy Clown."

"Dark vortex?" He arched a brow.

"Every little kid knows about the dark vortex. It's why we know not to go into closets or look under the bed."

"I don't think that's a real—"

"It's real."

"Lily, do you want me to look under the bed for you?" Nolan asked, his tone aggravatingly calm and reasonable.

She nodded. "Yes."

Nolan suppressed a grin. He lowered onto his hands and knees, threw the draped covers out of his way, and leaned close to the floor to look under the bed.

Lily felt a chill along her arm. She held her breath. Her eyes moved before her head turned.

She came face to forehead with a ghost.

He stood a couple inches from her face. When she glanced down, she saw his whiskers shift with a smile. "Boo!"

She gasped, jumping away from him.

The ghost crowed a high-pitched sound, holding his stomach and slapping his thigh as if it were the funniest thing in the world. "Oo-ee-ee-ee."

"I don't see anything," Nolan said, still looking under the bed.

The ghost of a miner grinned at her. He was shorter than her with a long, scraggly beard and wrinkles carved deep into his features like dry riverbeds in a desert. His gray hair curled around his ears with a flattened indent where his hat would have been.

"Uh, Nolan," Lily whispered.

"Nothing's here," Nolan said, pushing up from the floor.

"Nolan," she said louder, not taking her eyes off the ghost.

He stood. "What?"

Lily pointed at the transparent miner.

"What? You want to go?" Nolan asked.

"Ghost." Lily kept pointing.

"Stan," the ghost said. "Pleasure to meet ya, ma'am. Have ya seen a shoe anywhere? I can't seem to find where they put it."

"St-stan," Lily repeated. She glanced down but couldn't quite make out his feet against the wood floor.

"Stan? He's here?" Nolan sounded irritated as he walked to where she was pointing. He went through Stan's body. The ghost seemed to absorb into the man before reappearing on the other side. "Ask him where he put my truck."

"Eh-ee-ee-ee," was Stan's answer. He winked at her before disappearing.

"Well? What did he say? Where's my truck?" Nolan practically shouted as if that would make the ghost hear him better.

"He's gone."

"Did he say where?"

"No. He just laughed when you asked him. He's looking for a missing shoe though." Lily ran her hands through her hair and went to a dark window to look out over the backyard. The moon was bright but not full, casting shadows over the landscape. Below, she saw the figure of her aunt dancing in front of the barn, holding Herman over her head. She turned her back on the window. "My life is ridiculous, and I just saw my aunt Polly naked."

Chapter Ten

"What's with the gnomes?" Deputy Tegan Herczeg eyed the statues evenly spaced to encircle the house. Her long dark hair was pulled back into a ponytail and if she didn't have such a harsh expression, she would have been considered pretty. As it was, she was intimidating, made more so by the black uniform she wore.

"Decorating choice." Lily knew she didn't sound convincing. "The vandalism is around back. It started when we first arrived here almost two weeks ago. I didn't report it because I thought it might be kids being stupid."

Deputy Herczeg didn't wait to be shown as she strode through the yard. Scaffolding had been set up by the side of the house. Lily glanced up to where Nolan stood beside the roof looking down at her, his hands on his hips. She lifted her hand in greeting.

In the last several days, he'd been a great support—even as lights fell from the ceilings, as plaster crumbled from the walls, as hammers disappeared, and bricks disintegrated to dust at a single touch. Aunt Polly's repairs were nothing more than a glamour, magical paint that hid bigger problems.

Her inheritance was as she'd first feared—a mess to be cleaned up, crumbling at her feet. Yet, somehow, she didn't feel depressed about it. Work didn't scare her. The trust fund had the money to pay for it. She was building a home.

Correction. Lily was trying to build a home for her family. Someone was trying to stop her.

Regardless, she'd make sure everything was repaired the right way. Rather, she'd trust Nolan to see to things being repaired the right way, since she didn't know what she was doing.

Burn marks scorched the lawn, spray paint marred the siding, and now giant carved symbols had been cut into the side of the barn. How someone managed to saw five-feet holes into the wood without being heard was beyond her.

"Who'd you piss off?" Herczeg examined one of the holes and then placed her hand on the edge to lean inside.

"I'm told everyone," Lily said. "We're Goode-Crawfords. Everyone is mad at us."

Herczeg glanced back, a half smile on her face. "Yeah. True."

"They're wrong, though. I have nothing to do with bad luck. As you can see, I'm kind of suffering from some bad luck of my own."

The deputy sniffed the air and leaned forward. "Are you cooking something in there? What's that smell."

A loud creak sounded. Herczeg pulled her head out of the hole. The black cat darted from the opening and ran away. Lily eyed the barn in surprise as it continued to creak and snap.

"Move," Herczeg said. "Now."

"What?" Lily frowned at the order.

"Move!" Herczeg charged her, hooking her waist with her arm to force her back.

They stumbled together. She landed hard in the dirt. The deputy lay on top of her like a protective shield. The cracking became louder and Lily was able to peek under the deputy's arm to watch the barn fall into a pile of dust and debris. Splinters of wood rained over them.

When the sound stopped, Herczeg pushed back to sit on the ground. "I'm inclined to believe you about the bad luck."

"Lily!" Nolan ran into the backyard. "What happened? Are you all right?"

"Structural issues." Lily pointed at the garage. "Guess the vandal cut into a support beam."

"But I checked that." Nolan examined the debris pile. "It was stable. All it needed was a few two-by-fours to shore up the back wall and a coat of paint."

"I think you might have missed something. Doesn't look sturdy to me." Deputy Herczeg dusted off her black pants. "I'll write up a report and I will try to patrol out here when I get the chance, but I'd suggest you do your thing and take care of the protection yourself."

Lily couldn't believe what she was hearing. "Are you telling me to... protect myself?"

"I'm telling you to do whatever it is you witches do to take care of this problem. Cast some spells. Hold some séances. Throw magic glitter in the air." Herczeg sighed. "I'm not sure what you expect the law to do."

"Your job," Lily shot back in surprise. "Find whoever destroyed my barn."

"My job?" Herczeg crossed her arms over her chest. "My job is to protect the citizens of Lucky Valley. My job is to keep the Garry brothers from fighting over the same woman they had the bad luck of falling in love with because she's a siren, and to make sure Leda Bourreau doesn't get so upset she starts World War Three out of her kitchen, and to keep tourists from falling into sink holes that materialize in the middle of town, and—"

"I'm a citizen," Lily said. "I'm new, but this is my home now, and this is a real threat. Someone is vandalizing my property. I don't feel safe."

"You're a Goode."

"You're a cop."

"I'm a deputy."

"Then do your job. Find out who is doing this." Lily placed her hands on her hips and faced the taller woman. "Treat me like I'm not a Goode. Treat me like I'm a person who needs your help."

"I'll write a report." Herczeg walked toward her truck. The dented brown and white vehicle looked as if it had seen better days. Small, rusted bullet holes dotted the side near the passenger door, as if the Sheriff's Department seal had made for someone's target practice. Perhaps even more disturbing was the long scratch marks near the back tire. "Make sure you lock your doors, keep your cellphone on you at all times, and I recommend investing in an alarm system. Maybe get a dog. Some outside motion lights wouldn't hurt."

"Motion lights and a dog," Lily repeated in disbelief.

"You wanted the same advice I'd give a normal, everyday person, that's it." The deputy stopped as she opened the truck door. "I don't mean to sound insensitive, but we both know you're a Goode. You can take care of this yourself. I have citizens of this town with real problems who can't fight what's happening around here."

Lily shivered at the ominous statement.

Herczeg directed her attention to Nolan. "Councilman Rana was looking for you at the city building this morning. It seems no one has seen you down there for a few days."

"I picked up some extra work and haven't been in the office." Nolan answered. "I'll be sure to give him a call."

"We've been getting complaints of strange smells near the park. Goblins might be hoarding in their dens again. I'm sure he just wanted you to write them up," the deputy said.

"Yeah, I'm sure that's it," he answered, though there was something strange in the way he said it that made Lily wonder if she was missing something.

Herczeg climbed into her truck, began to back out to the end of the drive, only to pause and come forward again. Rolling down the window, she pulled a phone away from her ear and leaned out to look at Nolan. "You misplace your truck over in Unlucky?"

Nolan glanced at Lily. "Maybe."

"You want us to send a crew over to help you with that?" she asked.

Nolan flinched. "I'll figure it out."

"He's got it," Deputy Herczeg said into the phone. She listened to the caller's answer before laughing. "You don't say." She lowered the phone and said to Nolan, "Are you sure you don't want a crane?"

"Yeah, maybe I should," Nolan said.

"I'll let the tow company know." Herczeg drove away.

"A crane?" Lily asked.

"I'm almost too scared to look," Nolan said.

"Picnic," Polly called in excitement as she came out of the house. She wore a yellow and pink 1950s dress and a bright green sunhat with pink flowers. Her sunglasses and chunky plastic jewelry finished the look. Like always, the woman managed to make the quirky look fabulous. She had her arm looped in the handle of a covered basket. She paused by the sign-holding gnome. This time his message read, "Tulips."

Lily looked down at yet another of her jeans and t-shirt combinations. The more she was around Polly, the more she was beginning to think her own wardrobe was incredibly boring. Jesse was supposed to be mailing them extra clothes from Washington, but their little sister wasn't exactly happy with the fact they didn't come home. At least next to Nolan, she didn't appear out of place. Except for the first night he came to the house, the man lived in work boots, white t-shirts, and an occasional red flannel.

"Oh, I'm sorry, Aunt Polly," Lily said. "I don't think we have time for a picnic. The barn literally fell over, and the sheriff is having a crane do something to Nolan's truck, and—"

"And the tiddle-widdles don't widdle-tid, and the faddle-daddles don't faddle, and the goose doesn't quack," Polly waved her hand in the air as she walked toward Lily's sedan, "and the aliens don't land on Tuesdays."

Nolan had walked to town to pick up the car and drive it back. She knew she should have offered the vehicle so he could look for his truck, but he hadn't asked to borrow it and she didn't suggest it. With his truck missing, he had been staying at the house with them. It only made

Better Haunts and Garden Gnomes

sense. Lily felt safer with a werewolf bodyguard around.

"Polly, are you... all right?" Lily knew she'd asked the woman that a lot, but there were times when her behavior gave reason for concern.

"It's always something." Polly put the basket in the backseat. "You worry too much about little things that don't need you fretting over them. The barn isn't going to regrow itself. Until you and Florus find your powers, we won't have the magic for that, and the pile of boards will be there tomorrow. I made taquitos."

"Should I get Dante?" Lily took a step toward the house.

"No, he's tied up at the moment. Leave him be. That boy needs some alone time." Polly waved her hand and all of the car doors opened. "Get in."

Lily rubbed her temples. A picnic did sound better than cleaning up rubble. "Okay, but just for an hour——" The last word barely made it past her lips when she tripped and flew forward. She would have landed on the ground face first if not for Nolan catching her a few inches before making impact.

"Oh, sugar bee, bad luck still hasn't worn off, has it? I knew it was a risk giving you a half-stirred potion." Suddenly, Polly stopped. "The barn collapsed?"

"That's what I've been telling you."

"Oh, darn, that's where I was brewing the potion to help ward off bad luck for the townsfolk. It smells awful during the cooking process. Oh well. I guess I'll have to start from scratch." Polly patted Lily's head as Nolan helped her to stand. "You'd better not drive, or you'll take us right off a cliff."

Chapter Eleven

Nolan drove past the wooden sign leading down the dirt road toward the old mining town. Someone had spray-painted a red "Un" in front of the word "Lucky," and the name stuck. Even though the ghost town of Unlucky Valley was close to the new town of Lucky Valley, the citizens didn't venture here as an unspoken rule. Reasons ranged from fear of ghosts to fear of curses, to fear of being caught trespassing on Goode land by the unrested spirit of soul-stealing Marigold Crawford Goode.

Nolan had gone out to the site a few times, mainly to make sure it was safe enough for any tourists who wandered through, and to make sure the old mines were still boarded up. Other than him, he knew the sheriff did patrols at least once every couple of weeks. That's probably how they'd found his truck.

The ghost town wasn't much to look at. There was a main dirt street flanked by wood-plank sidewalks and business fronts. On one side, a general store butted up against a barbershop which pressed against a telegraph office. A small alleyway, big enough for walking through and little else, created a path to behind the buildings and what was left of the bunkhouses. Next came a saloon which shared a wall with a bank, and then a sheriff's office with a single jail cell on the inside. Across the street was a two-story hotel. Well, when it had actually had a floor on the second story, it was a two-story. Now it was a giant space with a really high ceiling. It spread out over half the length of the main thorough-fare where it adjoined stables and a blacksmith barn.

"It's in such good condition," Lily said. "I was expecting it to be hollowed-out frames and overgrown with weeds."

"The residents must take care of it," Polly said.

"Townsfolk don't come here," Nolan said. "Good craftsmanship, I guess."

"I meant Unlucky's residents," Polly

corrected. "Just because you're dead doesn't mean you have to lay on your backside all day."

"It kind of does mean that," Lily countered. Nolan glanced over to see her hide a smile. She was egging her aunt on.

"I know—we should give tours," Polly said. "I'll call my new business Polly's Mostly Magical Fantastical Foray into Mysterious Worlds of Wonder. That will make three businesses, and I'll be my own empire."

"Three?" Nolan inquired.

"Polly's Perfectly Magical Mystical Wondrous World of Wonders back in Maine. It's my magic shop. And then there's Polly's Perfectly Magical Mystical Maids, Mops, and Lollipops. I don't have any clients yet, but I will."

"They all sound perfectly magical," Nolan said.

"Oh, roll down the window," Polly exclaimed. The sound of tapping came from the backseat.

"Child locks." Lily pointed toward the driver's side door. He turned the locks off.

Polly hit the button to roll down the window and began waving. "Such a pretty dress!"

"Do you see…?" Nolan gripped the steering wheel, his entire body rigid as he watched for signs of the afterlife. His phone vibrated in his pocket, not for the first time that day. He didn't bother looking. Odds were, it was the same person. Councilman Nathan Rana wouldn't be happy with the fact Nolan avoided his calls.

"I don't see anything," Lily answered. "Just keep driving. This place is kind of creepy."

Polly rolled up the window and leaned forward to whisper, "Pretty dress, but that poor woman's head... *tsk, tsk*."

"Where do you think the ghost parked your truck?" Lily ignored her aunt's comment.

"The deputy mentioned the mines. They're a little past town." He tried to force himself to relax, but it was hard. "And somewhere that requires a crane."

His phone stopped vibrating, but that didn't make him any less aware of what the council expected him to do. At any other time, he would have enjoyed a drive through the country with Lily. He could do without a chaperone in the backseat, but a guy couldn't be picky.

The road leading to the mines became more treacherous as large rocks littered the ground. It was more of a suggested path than a road. He did his best to avoid any bumps as he wove the car toward the main entrance. The mine entrance was a hole in the side of a rock face, but after a few steps inside, there would be a several-hundred-feet drop into the old tunnels below. Men used to be hauled up and down by a platform with a pulley system.

"I feel a little sick to my stomach." Lily held her midsection. "I think I need you to pull over, please."

"They can be draining," Polly said.

"Who?" Lily turned around to look at her aunt.

"The residents."

"We're here." Nolan stopped the car. His phone vibrated again, and he knew he'd have to answer sooner rather than later. He stepped out of the car and leaned in the door to tell Lily, "You can stay here since you're not feeling well."

Nolan reached for his phone, unsure what he'd tell the man. Either he lied and said he still planned on running the Goodes out of town and his working at the house was part of his elaborate plan to do just that, or he told the truth and the town council decided to fire him for helping the enemy. Somehow saying, "I have a crush on the Goode witch and I'm sure you'll like her if you just give her a chance," didn't feel like a wise decision. He didn't have a trust fund to pay his bills. He needed his city job.

Not that he was surprised, but Lily didn't take his advice to stay in the car as she stepped out to follow him, still holding her stomach. She was the most hardheaded woman he'd ever met. Maybe that's why he liked her so much.

Nolan put his phone back into his pocket, unanswered.

"I don't see any residents." Lily turned in a circle. She examined their surroundings for ghosts. Nolan didn't sense anything either and figured Polly was just having fun at their expense.

When he didn't see his truck parked near the mine, he frowned. "There's a small quarry up ahead. They used the stone on some of the structures in town and it's left a pit."

"Oh, no, you don't think Stan drove your truck off a cliff, do you, and that's why they said you needed a crane?" Lily followed him as he climbed the rocky path to the top ledge.

Seeing ruts in the ground, he was pretty sure he knew what awaited him.

"Yeah." Nolan pointed to the tailgate sticking up from where his truck had lodged against the rock face. It hadn't crashed all the way down, but it had been driven into a protrusion and was wedged at an almost ninety-degree angle. "I think Stan drove it off a cliff."

"Oh, wow." Lily patted his arm. "I hope you have insurance."

"I don't know if my policy covers ghost possession," he said.

"You could report that it was stolen," she offered. "Then you don't have to say how it was stolen, or by who."

"Dammit." Nolan ran his hands through his hair. "I really liked that truck."

"Lay this out for me, dear." Polly handed Nolan a blanket.

"Polly, I don't think this is the right time for picnicking." Lily tried to intercept the blanket.

"It's fine. Let her have the picnic. There's nothing I can do about the truck now and I'm hungry," Nolan said.

"Exactly. Now come get some fried chicken." Polly gestured to a flat spot on the ground overlooking the quarry and wrecked truck. Nolan spread the blanket. Polly sat down and pulled out a food container from her basket.

"Do you think it's drivable?" Lily walked to the ledge closest to the vehicle. "Maybe the rock stopped its fall. The front end doesn't look too smashed up. Stan probably didn't bother to turn the engine off when he parked so it would have run itself out of gas. I'm not sure what that will do to an engine. Maybe it will be fine."

She sounded adorably hopeful. Nolan did not share that hope.

"We have potato salad, coleslaw, baked beans, potato chips, watermelon…" Polly was saying behind them. They ignored her as they both leaned to the side as if to get a better view of the truck.

"At least I know the deputy was joking when she said we'd need a crane. A tow truck should do it," Nolan said. "Dammit."

"…fried chicken, hamburgers, chicken taquitos, beef taquitos…"

"Maybe I can get the trust to pay for the repairs for you. You work for me, and it happened while you were helping me," Lily offered.

"…lemon cake, donuts, pancakes…"

"Couldn't hurt to ask," Lily continued. "The worst they can say is no."

"…tacos, mini pizzas, corndogs, butterscotch pudding, macadamia nut cookies, licorice…"

"Thank you, but…" Nolan tilted his head in question. "Did she say pancakes?"

They both turned toward Polly in unison. Somehow, the woman had managed to lay out a feast—more than should have been able to fit in her basket. Almost every inch of the large blanket was covered with food.

"…bacon, pork chops, and mashed pota-toes." Polly grinned. "Dig in."

"Polly, this is—" Lily started to speak.

"Oh, you're right. I almost forgot." Polly dug into her basket and pulled out a pie. "Cheeseburger pickle pie. It's a real thing."

"I was going to say this is too much food," Lily finished.

"Stuff and nonsense," Polly dismissed. "We need options, and I'm hungry."

"No seafood," Nolan teased.

"Herman is sensitive about seafood. I couldn't have him seeing me pack that into the basket." Polly looked as if the answer should have been obvious.

"Quite right," Nolan mumbled. He looked over the spread. "I'll take a pancake and bacon."

"Strawberries and whipped cream on top?" Polly held up a bowl of fruit.

"Sure," he agreed.

"Picnic pancakes," Lily muttered. "Now I've seen everything."

"Cheeseburger pickle pie for you?" Polly asked Lily.

"That would be a no." Lily laughed. "Not pregnant. Not eating whatever that is."

"Oh." Polly's expression fell as if disappointed. Lily reached for a water bottle and took a drink. "A baby would have been a joy, but I respect you wanting to take it slow with Nolan."

Water spewed from Lily's lips, landing to the side of the blanket. She looked in horror at Polly then Nolan. "But, no, we're not... I'm not... I mean we're not..."

Nolan wasn't sure how to take her stuttering denial. To stop her from trying to explain, he stated, "We are not dating. Ours is a working arrangement."

"Friends," Lily said weakly, looking at Nolan as if waiting for him to contradict her. "I would say we're friends."

"Yes. Friends." Nolan nodded. He wasn't being asked out on a date, but it was better than being called her employee, so he'd gladly take it.

Polly giggled. "Eat your taquitos before they get cold."

Nolan sat on a patch of grass near the blanket. Polly handed him a tall stack of pancakes covered in strawberries and whipped cream. Bacon encircled the pancakes around the edge of the plate. "Aunt Polly, you throw one heck of a picnic."

"If you think this is impressive, you should see me throw a séance party." Polly handed Lily a plate full of taquitos with a side of potato salad. "Here. All your favorites."

"How do you...?" Lily slowly took the plate. "Did Dante tell you that?"

"Always questioning." Polly shook her head. "That's your problem. You're always thinking thoughts."

"Thinking thoughts?" Lily arched a brow.

"Yes, thinking thoughts about things that don't matter. You need to feel your way a little more. Maybe then your powers would come back to you. Save room for cherry pie."

Lily gave Polly an insolent grin and bit into a taquito.

Chapter Twelve

Lily walked the boarded sidewalks of Unlucky Valley, hearing them creak under her feet. She wished she had her phone so she could send pictures to Jesse. Her sister would love exploring a ghost town. As it was, the only way she could talk to Jesse was if she borrowed Nolan's phone. She and Dante had ordered a couple of cheap replacement flip phones that still hadn't arrived.

After the picnic, Nolan had called the deputy to find out when the tow truck would be there. Since it was on its way and they were already there, it was easier to stay instead of heading back to the house.

She watched a black cat dart into the doorway of the bank. Nolan's citation had mentioned a cattery, but this was only the second cat she'd seen on Goode land since arriving.

Lily touched the stone-and-wood siding of the saloon. If she looked hard enough, she imagined she could see speckles of white paint that might have once been a sign. Since no one was around, she said to herself, "I can't believe I own a ghost town. What was Marigold thinking, leaving this to me?"

Technically, the trust was from her father's side of the family. Joseph Goode had died in a car wreck when Lily was young and so the caretaking of the property had passed to his wife, but the trust wouldn't have been as accessible to Marigold. The woman had barely been able to follow a road map, let alone navigate the inner workings of a complicated legal mess.

A shiver worked over her and she again felt ill. A spot of red amidst the drab brown caught her attention from across the street and she moved down the sidewalk, only to discover it was a garden gnome statue standing in front of the hotel.

"Okay, that's weird." Lily glanced around to see if anyone could have put it there. "I don't remember seeing you on the drive in."

The feeling of apprehension increased, and she didn't cross over to where the gnome stood.

She backed away slowly, keeping an eye on it as if the statue would move on its own. But it didn't.

Exploring the town alone might not have been a good call, and she now questioned the reason why she'd felt compelled to do it in the first place. Her steps quickened as she turned to jog down the sidewalk. She slowed near the old jail and glanced back. The gnome remained where it was.

She giggled to herself. "I'm being stupid. No one is here. No ghosts in this ghost town."

As if to contradict her words, she caught movement through the jail's door. Whatever it was appeared to be the size of an adult. She listened but didn't hear anything.

Lily stepped closer to the door and said to whatever spirits might be lurking around, "You should move on. Find a light or something. This is private property." She gave a self-mocking laugh and dropped the tone of her voice an octave. "There's a new sheriff in town, and I'm coming in armed with—"

"Okay, stop, I'm sorry," a woman's voice answered.

Lily screamed in surprise at the clear response, which prompted the woman to scream, which then made Lily scream a second time.

"I didn't mean any harm. I just needed a

place to sleep." A woman stepped out from behind the old bars of the jail cell where she'd been hiding in the shadows. Her hands lifted in front of her in a defensive gesture. She looked young, maybe early twenties. She was pretty, with a heart-shaped face, dark hair and brown eyes. Her hair was pulled back from her face into a ponytail, and there were remnants of faded red lipstick staining her lips.

Lily stepped into the room and moved to get a better view inside the cell. A red sleeping bag was laid out on the floor next to a hiking pack and various other camping items. "What are you doing in here?"

"I thought this was abandoned." The woman began gathering her belongings. "I'm sorry. I'll go. I didn't mean to trespass."

"Wait, who are you? Are you a hiker? Are you lost? I didn't see any other cars." Lily kept her distance from the stranger.

"Oh, sorry, Mara Edison." The woman gave a small smile as she rolled her sleeping bag.

"Lily Goode," Lily said.

"Lily?" Nolan called. "Lily, where are you? What happened?"

Lily stepped out of the jail. "I'm fine. Mara startled me."

"Mara?" He glanced over her shoulder. He

looked as if he'd partially shifted to run to get to her and the fur was receding into his flesh. His eyes still carried a little bit of a glow.

"A hiker." Lily turned just in time to see Mara come up beside her. She watched to see if Nolan's shift had frightened her, but the woman didn't seem to notice it. Mara pulled the straps of her pack over her shoulders.

"Squatter, actually," Mara said. "I didn't have anywhere else to stay, and I didn't think anyone would care. I mean, the lady at the diner said no one ever comes out to Unlucky Valley. I thought it'd be all right, and better than sleeping out in the open."

"It's fine, you're not in trouble." Lily glanced around. "Actually, it's not fine. You can't live out here."

"I understand. I'll be on my way." Mara nodded before moving to leave.

Lily shared a look with Nolan before calling, "Are you hungry? We have an obscene amount of food."

Mara turned and looked interested. "I don't want to be a bother."

"No bother. Trust me. My aunt would love it if you joined us. Please." Lily gestured for the woman to follow them. "Come get something to eat."

"Lily, you don't know anything about this woman," Nolan whispered.

"Look at her. She's homeless. She probably hasn't eaten." Lily tugged at his arm to get him to walk with her. "She clearly needs help."

"When are you going to comprehend that Lucky Valley is not like other places?" He kept his voice low. "Nothing here is what it appears to be. That sweet innocent girl you're trying to save, yes, she could be human, or a bunnyshifter, or have some cute little trick where she can change the temperature of a room by a few degrees at will. Or that poor, starving homeless woman could be a big catshifter and you just found her den, or a vampire—"

"It's daylight," Lily dismissed.

"That proves my point. You don't even know that all vampires aren't allergic to sunlight. There are different kinds of vampires—psychics, dream feeders, night stalkers—"

"Not a vampire. Just a glow stick. I light up like a nightlight," Mara called from behind them. "And I have really great hearing, but that's not a supernatural genetic trait so much as a me trait."

"See, she's fine," Lily said.

"I am homeless and starving, though," Mara walked faster, catching up to them. "That part you got right. I haven't had a decent meal in months. There are some wild wood strawberries nearby though. They're small, but not bad. And prickly pear cactus."

"Are you from around here?" Lily asked. "I mean, you said you have superpowers."

"Glowing is not a superpower," Mara said. "Do you know how hard it is to find a boyfriend who's afraid of the dark and doesn't mind me glowing when I'm having nightmares?"

"I've never seen you in town. Where are you from?" Nolan's voice was a little gruff, and she wondered why Mara had put him on edge.

"Albuquerque," Mara answered.

"What are you doing here?" Nolan sounded more like an interrogator.

If Mara noticed his tone, she didn't let on. "I heard rumors that there were freaks like me, and I came to check it out. It's not a surprise that no one really likes to talk about the supernatural."

"How long are you staying?"

"Don't know." Mara adjusted her backpack. "How do you like being a shifter? I mean, that's what you are, right? I saw the fur and the fangs and the glowy eyes."

"I like the glowy eyes," Lily inserted, trying to lighten the conversation.

"It's fine." Nolan placed his hand on the back of Lily's arm and walked faster, forcing her to quicken her pace. "Polly will be worried about us."

"For an abandoned town, this sure is a busy place today," Mara said. "Truck's coming."

Nolan frowned. "You can hear that?"

Mara shrugged. "I told you, I have great hearing."

Lily looked behind them. "Hear what? I don't hear anything."

"Tow truck is close." Nolan lifted his hand and waved toward where Polly sat on the hood of Lily's car, her face toward the sunlight. "Polly, we have a hungry traveler passing through."

Polly slid off the car. She turned, dusting her skirt. The smile fell a little as she looked at Mara. "Hello."

"Hi." Mara lifted her hand in a quick greeting. Her lips pressed together as she glanced around the area.

"Lily, sugar bee, be a dear and get my basket. There should be a sandwich left in there," Polly said.

Mara shrugged out of her pack and propped it against a rock.

Lily chuckled as she went to open the basket's lid. "Don't be silly. I'm sure there's more than a sand...wich."

She was wrong. In the basket that should

have been overflowing with leftovers rested a single sandwich wrapped in plastic. It wasn't even an amazing sandwich, like she'd expect inside Polly's basket, but two pieces of sliced bread with a thin layer of meat and cheese inside.

She reached in to grab it. "I guess I was wrong. We just have a sandwich left."

"Turkey," Polly said.

"Oh, ah, thanks." Mara reached to take it but didn't open it like a woman who hadn't eaten in a while. "Actually, I'm allergic to turkey, so thank you anyway, but…" She handed the sandwich back.

Dust lifted in the distance, announcing the arrival of the tow truck.

"Oh, I'm sorry to hear that," Polly said. "Well, I'm sure the tow truck driver can give you a lift into town. There's food there."

Lily crossed to her aunt and took her by the arm. She pulled her aside and whispered, "Polly, what's wrong with you? Where did all the food go? Why won't you give her something to eat? The poor girl is starving."

"I offered food. She didn't want it."

Lily gripped the plain sandwich so tightly that the bread smashed in the plastic. She held it up. "Why won't you give her something to eat that won't throw her into anaphylactic shock? I know we haven't known each other for long, but this doesn't seem—"

"You think too much," Polly said. "You should feel more."

"Feel what? Empathy for a hungry girl who is alone in the world, trying to take care of herself? Trust me, I know what that's like. I wish someone would have stopped to offer me food." Lily forced Polly to meet her gaze. "Is she a paranormal threat? Is she a face melting creature? Or a troll-goblin hybrid?"

"Well, no…"

"Okay, so as long as she's not posing any kind of supernatural danger, I think we should check your basket again. Maybe I missed something."

Polly sighed and nodded. "Yeah, maybe there's some leftover cheeseburger pickle pie."

"Polly!" Lily scolded at the horrible suggestion.

"I mean a hamburger," Polly said.

"Thank you." Lily went back to the basket and opened it. She dropped the squished sandwich inside and pulled out a foil-wrapped burger. "I must have missed this. Can you have hamburgers?"

"Oh, yes, my favorite." Mara reached for it an unwrapped it. She bit into and said with a mouthful, "*Mm, mank mou.*"

"You're welcome," Lily answered. She arched a brow at Nolan and Polly. What the heck was wrong with them? They were acting weird. She might be the only non-supernatural in the group, but Lily knew to trust her instincts when it came to judging people. Her intuition had served her well in the past. Mara reminded Lily of her younger self. People had been inclined not to like Lily when she was Mara's age. She'd also been a little rough around the edges, but understandably so since she'd carried so much distrust and fear.

"Excuse me. I'm going for a stroll. I need to talk to the flowers." Polly didn't wait for an answer as she left, but her steps lost their usual pep.

"Should I go?" Mara asked, wiping her mouth on the back of her hand. "I didn't mean to upset anyone."

"It's not you. Polly is just... different." Lily tried to excuse the behavior.

The arrival of the tow truck interrupted the awkward situation. The words "Taylor Towing" were spelled out in bright green paint on the door.

Nolan went to greet the man who stepped out of the truck. "Hey, Colt, the family finally rope you into the business or did you flunk out of medical school?"

"Is it true you tried to drive yourself off a cliff?" Colt looked as if he'd been body-jacked from a tropical island and transplanted in Colorado. His dark hair wound into dreadlocks, falling to his shoulders. He wore a t-shirt and jeans with work boots, but somehow, she pictured him with a Hawaiian shirt on a beach.

"Who's the hottie?" Mara whispered.

As if hearing her, Colt grinned in their direction.

"Colt, this is Lily Goode, and…" Nolan motioned at Mara as if he didn't remember her name.

"Mara Edison, drifter," Mara filled in.

Lily furrowed her brow at Nolan. Why was he being so rude? There was definitely something up. Maybe Nolan and Polly needed an after-picnic nap.

"Mara is staying with us at our new bed and breakfast," Lily blurted, not knowing why she'd said it. She touched Mara's arm, but the woman stiffened in surprise and pulled away as if on reflex.

"Where's the truck?" Colt asked. Nolan pointed toward the cliff and they walked in that direction. "There's a new bed and breakfast?"

"No. Well, maybe." Lily followed them. "I'm considering changing the Goode house into one.

I might as well make something useful out of my inheritance."

Colt's head fell back, and he laughed before realizing Lily was serious. The sound stopped as quickly as it started. "You want people to visit the Goode house? Willingly? And sleep there?"

"Why not?" Lily asked.

"It's the Goode house." Colt looked at Nolan for support.

"There's plenty of room," Nolan answered. "Tourism would be good for town businesses."

"Is that a truck down there? What the hell happened?" Mara exclaimed.

"Stolen," Lily answered.

"Bad brakes," Nolan said at the same time.

"Okay," Mara drawled, clearly not believing them.

Lily shot Nolan a questioning look.

"It's not a lie. The brakes didn't work when Stan…" He let his words trail off so as not to reveal too much.

Colt knelt and placed his hand on the ground for balance as he studied the situation. "I'll give you one thing, Nolan, when you mess up, you mess up real good."

"I do what I can." Nolan widened his stance as he looked over the edge.

"Wait, are you the lady Patrick and Luke

chased up a tree?" Colt asked. Lily's expression must have answered for her because he whistled softly and shook his head. "When they said a new Goode was in town, I was expecting…"

"Warts and broomstick?" Lily asked.

"Something like that." Colt grinned. It was obvious the man was a charmer, and she couldn't help but return the smile. "You're not old and warty at all."

"Aren't you scared of me?" Lily challenged.

"Should I be?"

"I'm told Goodes are scary. We steal souls and bring about bad luck."

Colt stepped closer. "I'll let you steal anything you want from me."

Lily heard Nolan clear his throat, and she blinked in surprise, realizing she'd been flirting. Flirting? She didn't flirt. Her head felt a little fuzzy, and she closed her eyes.

"You going to get this truck out of the quarry or do we need to call one of your brothers to help you?" Nolan asked, stepping between Lily and Colt. She frowned at his back.

"So, is that Nolan guy like your boyfriend?" Mara asked.

"No," Lily denied. "I mean, he's a boy and we're friends and—"

Mara laughed. "Okay, if you say so, but I

think someone should probably let him know if you're not together." She took another bite of her burger, finishing it, and wadded the foil into a ball.

When Mara lifted her arm to throw her trash into the quarry, Lily held her hand to block her from littering. "Let me take care of that for you."

Mara tossed the foil at her instead.

The sound of the tow truck prompted her to move out of the way as Colt backed toward the edge. Nolan ran behind the truck and directed Colt into place before yelling, "Stop."

"Did you mean what you said about me staying with you?" Mara asked.

Lily kept her eyes on the tow truck, watching as the men climbed on the back and began discussing how they were going to solve the problem of hooking the vehicle so they could pull it up.

"Sure. We're in construction, but there's plenty of space and it's better than that old jail cell." Lily didn't really think of her response. "You'll at least have a bed and people to talk to."

"I can't pay," Mara insisted.

Lily glanced at the woman. Her brown eyes seemed wary, even as she kept a neutral expression. "I'm not asking you to."

"I'm not charity."

"Then help out while you're there." Lily wasn't worried about it.

Nolan and Colt were having an animated conversation about how to proceed, which included them acting out their plans.

"I don't understand why you're being nice to me," Mara's voice was soft compared to the men's.

Nolan touched his waist and then dove his hands up and over as if to indicate he would be lowered over the edge. Lily's breath caught at the idea and she rushed forward to stop it.

"Can't we just fish it out like a hook on a string?" She motioned toward the giant boom attached to the back of the tow truck.

Both men looked at her like she was crazy.

"What fun is that?" Colt shook his head.

"So if we tie off a rope, I can lower myself down and hook the—" Nolan began.

"No. I'll lower myself—" Colt interrupted.

"It's my truck."

"It's my hook."

"Never mind," Lily muttered backing away. "Don't come yelling for me when you're falling down the side of a cliff."

Chapter Thirteen

"I can't talk now. You need to stop calling." Nolan said into his phone, keeping his voice low. He stood in the mudroom by the back door and considered taking his call into the basement as not to be overheard. "It's not a good time."

"Don't speak, just listen." Councilman Rana's tone held authority. He'd been in a position of power in Lucky Valley since Nolan was a kid. "The evacuation plan is not coming along as quickly as we had hoped. Do I need to remind you that we are on a time limit? If they stay in that house for too long, they city will not be able to consider it abandoned property. The countdown clock will reset, and we'll have to wait another five years before we can legally seize it and knock it down. It's time the city of Lucky

Valley moved past its tragic history with the Goode and Crawford families."

Nolan glanced into the kitchen to see if anyone was coming.

"There is some concern that you've been compromised by the witches," Rana said.

"I have not," Nolan stated.

"Them prove it. Stop playing house and get——"

"I have to go," Nolan interrupted in a rush before he disconnected the call. His sense of duty to the town warred with how he felt about Lily Goode. Was he under her spell? He had a hard time believing she was such a great actress that she hid evilness from him. Then again, a siren could make someone do whatever they wanted by invoking feelings of love and security.

Nolan gripped his hammer as he moved to look out the back window at the fallen barn. Someone had taken the gnomes and lined them up to spell the word "ours." He'd about had it with those stupid statues, always popping up when he was trying to work, tripping him, staring at him with those beady eyes and forever happy smiles.

"I've thought about doing the same thing," Lily said, joining him, "but trust me, you don't want to bring down Aunt Polly's wrath if you smash her gnome friends with a hammer. She loves playing with those things. They're like her dolls."

Lily wore an eighties rock band t-shirt and was in the process of pulling her hair back into a bun.

"I never see her move them. Do you think she's using magic?" Nolan wasn't completely familiar with the rules of magic, but after seeing the unscientifically large picnic come out of a small basket, he wouldn't be surprised by Polly's abilities.

"You're asking the wrong Goode. Apparently, I couldn't find my powers if they jumped up and bit me in the hindquarters." She gave a small laugh.

"Do you want to find them?" He tapped the end of the hammer against the wood frame of the windowsill without causing any damage. It was more of a nervous tick.

"I feel like there's a piece of me just out of my reach. It's like a word on the tip of my tongue, or a melody I can start but not finish, someone's name I can't remember but should." She patted her hair, checking to see if all the strands were pulled back. "Is Colt really taking a break from medical school?"

Nolan frowned, not liking the question. "Sure."

"Have you known him long?"

"He's a siren. You should stay away from him until you're married," Nolan warned. "His voice lures unattached women."

"But he's a he," Lily debated.

"Not all sirens are girls." Nolan wanted to change the subject. "Where's your new friend?"

"I sent her up to the third floor to pick an empty room." Lily's hand glided over his and she gently tried to pry the hammer from his grip. "You don't like her very much."

It wasn't a question.

A splash sounded, and they both glanced to Polly's pet lobster. Herman rested in a cake pan filled with water on the kitchen counter. A small beret sat on his head. If lobsters had chins, it would be resting on the side of the pan. It appeared as if the crustacean was watching them.

Nolan let her take the tool from him. "You are aware that your household is weird, aren't you?"

"Yeah, but it's kind of a cool-weird, isn't it?" She placed the hammer on the counter and smiled at Herman. "You look very dapper today, sir."

"I don't trust Mara." Nolan couldn't keep the opinion to himself. He liked Lily—and not just her bizarre family and crazy life. He *liked* her. She was stubborn and hard-headed and guarded with her emotions. She was frustrating and contrary and sometimes made jokes when she shouldn't. But she would do anything for those she cared about. For all her flaws, she had great strengths. She was kind, and loyal, and he liked her. A lot. More than a lot.

"You don't know her."

"Neither do you—"

A sharp scream sounded from upstairs.

Lily grabbed his arm. "We didn't tell her about the ghosts."

Nolan ran across the house and up the stairs.

Mara came around the corner, saw them and instantly backed away. She held up her fists, ready to fight as her eyes darted around. Finding an antique candlestick, she grabbed it and wielded it like a bat. "Stay away from me!"

"Mara, I'm sorry, it's just Stan. He's ornery, but he doesn't mean harm, I don't think," Lily tried to explain. "I think he just wants his shoe."

"What kind of place is this? Why do you have a man tied up in the attic? Is that what you do? Find drifters off the road and lure us here and..." She swung the candlestick in warning, even though no one approached her.

"What are you talking about? What man?" Lily asked.

"The dead guy tied up in the attic. I saw... I saw..." Mara shook, unable to finish her sentence.

"Dead guy?" Lily pushed past Nolan before he could grab her. "Dante? Dante, answer me!"

The panic in her voice was clear, and Nolan ignored Mara as he chased after Lily. He caught up to her by a third-story bedroom door. "Lily—"

"Where's Dante? Polly said my brother was tied up and couldn't go with us today, but I thought that was a figure of speech." Lily frantically moved to the next bedroom, and then the next. Finding all four empty, she said, "Attic." Lily looked at the ceiling. "She said attic. There has to be an access panel somewhere."

Then Lily looked at the small door at the top of the stairs.

Nolan was closer and beat her to it. He pulled the door open only to find Dante bound to a wooden chair. His ankles were tied to the legs, and his hands were pinned at his sides by the thick rope holding him against the back of the seat. He was surrounded by lit candles. Herbs were sprinkled on the floor. The smell was pungent, even without his shifter senses.

"Dante!" Lily tried to move past Nolan, but he blocked her.

Dante wasn't moving, and his skin had a blue cast. Nolan didn't want her to see this. "Lily, I don't think you should—"

"He's my brother," she cried as she pushed past him. She grabbed Dante's face. "He's cold. We need to warm him up. He's got something on his skin. It's sticky."

"Don't move him," Polly called from below. "He's like a half-baked cookie. He needs more time."

"What did you do to him, Polly?" Lily's eyes begged him for help and Nolan couldn't refuse. "Don't let her hurt him. We need to get him to the hospital. His body temperature is too cold."

"You can't move him." Polly tried to push her way into the crowded room. "He's not done."

"Listen, witch, we're not putting my brother into your oven after you fatten him up with cookies." Lily tugged at Dante's ropes. "I've read that fairytale and that's not how this story ends, so you go find some other cookies because you can't have my brother."

"You don't know what you're doing," Polly

protested. She tried to grab Nolan's arm, but he shrugged her off.

"Nolan, give me a knife. We need to get him out of here," Lily insisted, digging her fingers in a knot with little progress.

He didn't carry a knife, but he didn't really need one. He let his hand shift. Sharp claws extended from his fingertips, and he began swiping them against the rope to fray it apart.

"I'm calling his powers. Marigold never should have separated you from your magic." Polly went around the edge of the room and patted Dante on the head. "He's not dead. He's only half dead. It's the only way to spark them into coming to help him. He knew what we were doing. I only tied him up so he couldn't wander off and hurt himself. These things can be disorientating. I know his magic is here somewhere. We just need to force it to come out from hiding."

"Why would you tell Dante about this and not me?" Lily pushed Polly's hand off her brother's head. "It's too dangerous. Look at him. I can't lose him. Nolan, please, I can't lose him."

"You're unlucky right now. If I gave you this potion, bad luck says it would kill you before you received your powers. It's the same reason you shouldn't be in here."

A chattering sound interrupted them, followed by scratching in the wall.

"What is that?" Lily asked.

Nolan focused his hearing to listen to what sounded like a large rodent.

"Don't stop." Lily hit his shoulder. He clawed harder. The ropes were thick, and he could only snag a few of the tough strands at a time.

"Stop," Polly whispered, holding up her hand. He paused long enough to see the rope healing itself as if he'd never frayed it. "It's coming."

Lily grabbed his arm and squeezed tightly. Nolan automatically pulled her against him as they listened to the sound move along the wall, only to drop toward the floor. A floorboard lifted and fell in a steady tapping rhythm, *tap, tap, tap,* held in place by old nails. With each beat, Lily's grip tightened, and the board pushed higher.

Lily reached for her brother's chair and tried to drag it toward the door. The legs scraped and caught on the old planks.

"I'll carry him," he decided, reaching to lift the man and chair to get Dante out of there. The chair wouldn't leave the floor, no matter how hard he tried to move it.

The board finally snapped free. Nolan grabbed Dante by the arms, unable to keep his eyes off the new hole in the floor. The chittering started from within.

Suddenly, a furry head poked up. Lily gasped and shook, making a strangled noise of fright. A fat raccoon pulled itself out of the hole and sat up, rubbing his hands together.

"That's the same pest that was living in the old trunk," Lily said.

"This is good," Polly said. "It's meant to happen. It's working."

"That thing probably has rabies," Lily answered, tugging harder. "Nolan, help me!"

The raccoon hissed at Lily as if he understood her. A yellow flash of light came out of the animal.

Nolan tried to pull Lily out of the way as the beam was aimed at her chest. The light followed her, striking her in the back and causing her to fall against him hard. Her eyes widened in pain as they met his. His foot slid back, hitting the wall seconds before the rest of his body. Nolan's head hit a beam in the slanted ceiling and he felt a sharp jab in the back of his arm. Pain raced down his body and he couldn't immediately push away. He held Lily against him.

The raccoon leapt onto Dante's lap and grabbed the man's face. The animal screeched, and another yellow light shot out of its mouth. It hit Dante between the eyes.

Lily's brother inhaled sharply and strained against his ties. The chair tipped but then righted itself. Dante gasped, his mouth stretching wide as he breathed hard. His blue coloring corrected itself and his skin darkened.

"There he is. There's my fully baked cookie," Polly said. "All this time, the naughty raccoon had stolen your magic. No wonder I couldn't locate it." She faced the raccoon who stood on Dante's lap. The animal tapped its paws against Dante's cheeks, chattering. "You've been carrying it all over the house, you sneaky thief, leaving magic in the walls."

Lily shivered in his arms. Nolan tried to release her, but she slumped, and he had to hold her upright. Each movement made him aware of a sharp object in his shoulder. In order to see to the wound, he'd have to let her go. He couldn't.

"What's happening?" Nolan asked. "What's wrong with Lily?"

"The potion I gave her to spread out the bad luck is still affecting her. The fact she came in here at the moment she did, and the way her powers were returned to her like a flying raccoon loogie, well... all clearly bad luck. Hopefully not fatal, but definitely not good." Polly pet the raccoon who in turn hissed at her. She snatched her hand back. "Well, aren't you the temperamental one?" She laughed. "It looks like Dante's familiar has found him."

"Polly, I need you to help Lily," Nolan said. When she didn't move fast enough, he added louder, "Polly, take her."

His arm fell to his side. Lily swung away from him at an odd angle as he tried to prop her up. Polly braced Lily under the arm and took the weight off him. As Polly eased Lily to the floor, Nolan grit his teeth and pried himself from the wall. He turned to find an exposed nail sticking out from the wood. The thick metal had been hammered through the wall, and when he'd fallen against it, he'd impaled his shoulder.

His arm tingled, and something trickled down his back and leg. When he examined the wall, he found it wasn't just one nail, but a line of them, spaced evenly apart. They'd also stabbed his back and thigh. Awareness made the wounds throb in pain.

"Someone get this thing off me before it gives me rabies," Dante said through gritted teeth. His legs jerked, but the restraints kept him locked in the chair. The raccoon had his face a few inches from Dante's and the man couldn't move away.

Nolan grabbed his side. It became hard to

breathe. He dropped to his knees. A gnome statue stood in the doorway, watching them.

Polly left Lily on the floor. She grabbed the raccoon around the waist from behind and lifted him from Dante's lap. The animal hissed and flailed his arms and legs, trying desperately to go back.

Before he knew what was happening, he was on the floor next to Lily, still clutching his side. She was unconscious, but her chest lifted with breath. He tried to wake her by touching her cheek. She was warm against his fingers as they slid over her skin. A smear of blood was left behind.

Lily's closed eyes faced him. His hand slid to rest on her neck, and he felt her pulse beat against his fingertips. With each beat, his vision dimmed. He vaguely saw movement behind her. The raccoon clung to Dante's leg as the man thrashed violently against the restraints. The chair lifted off the ground, levitating.

"An overbaked cookie, a burnt cookie, and a broken one. This batch is not coming out well at all," Polly said.

Chapter Fourteen

"I can't believe you levitated a chair," Lily said to her brother. "And I can't believe I missed it."

She stood at the window looking into the hospital room where Nolan rested. Behind them, a nurse pushed a cart. The squeaky wheel marked her slow progress. They waited until she passed.

"If I hadn't experienced it for myself, I would have never believed we could do magic. We're witches. We're freaking witches." Dante's answer was soft. "How cool is that!"

"Speak for yourself. I blew up a lightbulb," Lily grumbled as she gestured at Nolan, "and nearly killed the only contractor willing to work with us."

"Yeah, your superpowers kinda suck," Dante teased.

"You kinda suck," she answered.

"You can go in. It's not locked," a woman interrupted. Lily turned to the nurse with the cart. Her pink scrubs were decorated with happy bunnies. Short dark hair framed her face in a pixie cut though she was far from pixyish.

"We don't want to wake him," Lily said.

"Hearing friends might do him some good." The nurse grabbed a box of gloves off the cart and stepped into another room.

"Don't look at me, he's your friend," Dante said. "I'm not the one who broke him."

"Yeah, you're just the one who made out with a raccoon." Lily pushed open the door but didn't enter the room.

"Oh, hey, no," Dante protested. "Polly had me tied up."

Lily arched a brow. "Do you think that makes it any less funny? You were tied up by an old lady and your spirit animal is a raccoon."

"I dare you to call her old to her face," Dante challenged.

There was no way Lily was insulting Polly. Besides, it was impossible to tell exactly how old her aunt was. "I dare you to use your powers to materialize me a cheeseburger and fries."

"I dare you to go in there and talk to your boyfriend." Dante pushed the door open wider and motioned that she should go in.

"Aren't you coming?" Lily took one step in and stopped.

"No. Got any cash on you?"

"No. I left my purse at home," Lily said. Dante let go of the door. "Where are you going?"

"I'm going to use my powers and find a cheeseburger." The weighted metal bumped into her and forced her to move aside. It closed her in the room. Dante strolled away, presumably in search of the cafeteria.

Lily stared at Nolan. The view wasn't any better inside the room. His pasty complexion didn't put her at ease.

"The doctors said you're very lucky. The nail in your back missed your kidney, and the others missed major arteries. You bruised your lungs. I tried to tell them you hit a wall, but they don't believe me. They said it looks like you fell from a height. They irrigated the wounds but said they didn't give you stitches because that might seal in bacteria."

He still slept.

"They gave you a tetanus shot," Lily continued, unsure what else to say to him. "I'm not sure why they told me all that, but I guess it's because we brought you in."

Still nothing.

"Some council guy kept calling your phone. It might be urgent. Caller ID said Councilman Rana. I didn't answer. It's probably work stuff anyway. I almost forgot you had another job besides dealing with my madhouse."

Lily glanced around the room. Aside from the bed, portable tray table, and a wall of machines, there wasn't anything decorative—not even a television. "I have to tell you, this room looks like a prison cell. Not very pretty."

"It is a cell. There's a button on the outside that locks it down. They're worried I'll go all werewolf on them," Nolan mumbled. His eyes had a glassy sheen as they met hers. "And they're telling you because you're a Goode, and they're scared you'll curse them if they don't give you what you want."

"You heard that?"

"Cheeseburger, tetanus, work, prison, I'm your hero and you don't know what you'd do without me." His lip twitched. "Yeah, I heard you."

"Something like that." Lily found herself going to his bedside and touching his forehead, as if that might tell her more than the doctors. He felt warm. "How do you feel?"

He lifted the hand that had the IV in it. "Hydrated."

"They gave you something for the pain."

"It's working. It doesn't hurt. How are you?"

She slid her hand to his cheek. "Apparently, I have my magic back. I think I set off all the car alarms in the parking lot without touching them, so there's that."

The corner of his lip curled into a half smile. "I can see why the doctors are scared of you."

"It's strange. I feel full, like I had a giant meal, but I'm hungry. My body knows the magic is supposed to be there, but my mind is just… I'm not making sense, am I?"

"Not really." Nolan eyed his hand and then the bag he was attached to. "Do me a favor. Is the warden still out there?"

"Warden?"

"Ulga. The ogre in the bunny scrubs." Nolan nodded toward the door. He threw the covers off his lap. The blue hospital gown revealed his naked legs and bare feet. "Do you see my clothes?"

"I don't think you should move around like that." Lily tried to push him back into bed. Her hand pressed against his chest.

"I'm fine. Hospitals make me edgy." He didn't lay down. Her hand began to tingle, aware of his heart beating beneath it.

She pushed harder, trying to force him to relax. "Nolan, you need your rest. I'm not sneaking you out before the doctors clear you."

Suddenly, he fell back, and she went with him. Lily landed against his chest, her hand trapped between their bodies. His heat infused her. The hospital gown did not provide much of a barrier between them.

"Nol—"

The word never made it past her lips. He kissed her, his mouth pressing tightly to hers. She gasped in surprise but didn't pull away. The tingling intensified. His grip tightened on her waist. Her hand slid from his chest to his face and she felt her body turning to lay back on the soft bed.

Nolan's body half covered her in a protective cocoon. The kiss deepened, and she couldn't think beyond that perfect moment. He caressed her face, his thumb running along her lower lip as he pulled away. They breathed hard, their breaths mingling in the close proximity.

"I won't apologize," he whispered.

"I won't ask you to." Something tickled her neck, and she gasped to realize they were in an open field and the bed was grass. The hospital IV stand stood beside them, still connected to his hand. "How…? Where are we?"

Nolan glanced around, not as surprised as she was. "Thanks for the escape. That was easier than I thought it would be."

"I did this?" She pushed up and he let her sit. Mountain peaks dotted the skyline, and the valley stretched for miles. There was no sign of civilization. "Oh, crap, what are we going to do? I don't even know where we are."

"It looks familiar…" He stood and turned in a circle. The IV tubing wrapped his legs, and he frowned before pulling the IV from his hand.

"You might need that," Lily said. "We don't have any supplies and—"

"Relax," he soothed. "I'm more worried about not having clothes to cover my naked backside."

"Nolan, I'm not joking. This is serious. I don't know how I brought us here. I didn't want you to leave the hospital. I wanted the doctors to finish checking you out. Everyone is right. My powers are bad luck."

"I recognize this valley. We're only about ten miles away from the mines. It's fine. We can walk that." He reached down to help her to her feet.

"But your leg. They said the puncture

wounds were several inches deep. You should be taking it easy."

"Do you think you can control your powers enough to get us back to the house?"

She shook her head.

"Then we walk. It's that simple."

"Should we take that IV bag with us?"

"It's saline. I don't think drinking it is advisable. It would be like drinking salt water. And I'm not going to try to insert that needle into our hands." Nolan motioned that she should walk.

"You don't even have shoes."

"I have werewolf feet."

"Are you sure you can walk?"

"Can we go before I sunburn my backside?"

Lily automatically glanced down his body. The hospital gown offered little protection, and she could see the outline of his form through the material from the bright sunlight. She nodded and began to walk the way he'd indicated.

After they'd moved several feet, with Nolan walking behind her, she said, "You kissed me."

"I'm still not apologizing for that."

Lily glanced back and smiled. "I'm not asking you to."

Chapter Fifteen

"Where have you been?" Dante stood on the front porch with his arms crossed over his chest. Next to him, the sign gnome held an empty sign. "Do you know how worried I've been? I thought someone kidnapped you. Deputy Do-Nothing told me there was nothing they could do because you were an adult and a Goode. I wanted to hex her, but Polly didn't let me."

Lily was too exhausted to argue with her brother. Trekking ten miles through mountain valleys and trees wasn't the same as ten miles on a straight sidewalk. At least they'd made it back before nightfall. Her throat was parched, and she wanted nothing more than to collapse into a cool bath. "We're fine. We had a slight magical mishap."

"You should have called," Dante insisted.

"No phone," Nolan answered for her. "Move out of her way. She needs water."

"Nice dress," Dante teased.

"Leave him alone, Florus." Lily tried to walk into the house.

Dante stepped aside but grabbed her arm. "I thought something happened to you."

"It did, but I'm fine." She patted his shoulder. He didn't let go. "I magically transported us to nowhere, and we walked twenty-thousand miles to get back. I also think I caused a rockslide and an animal uprising."

"The elk stampede wasn't your fault," Nolan said, "and that wasn't a rockslide."

"It was," she mouthed to her brother.

"Your superpowers really do suck." Dante let her go.

"Yeah, they are not cool." Lily made her way toward the kitchen for a drink. A row of garden gnomes blocked the hallway so she turned into the living room to avoid stepping over them. Chattering caught her attention, but she was too tired to be startled by the raccoon lounging on her broken antique couch, and she kept walking to the kitchen sink.

Lily turned on the water, leaned over, and drank straight from the stream coming from the faucet. Everything ached—her heels, her ankles, her calves, her brain. Feeling more than seeing Nolan behind her, she moved away from the running faucet to give him a turn. When he leaned over, the back of his thigh became exposed and she forced herself to look away.

"All I want is a bottle of wine and a bath—" Lily's words ended sharply as she looked through the kitchen window. A flashlight beam danced in the shadows, shining over the barn debris while hiding whoever carried it. "Someone's in the backyard."

She leaned closer to the window.

A figure came from below, jumping in front of the window. She yelped in surprise before realizing it was the black cat.

"I don't see anyone," Nolan said, his eyes shifted.

"By the barn. There's a..." Lily pointed out the window but there was nothing there.

"Stay here. I'll go look." Nolan tried to go outside to investigate, but she stopped him by grabbing hold of his hospital gown sleeve.

"You can't go out in that outfit." She stared at the window, watching for the light. "There, by the barn. Do you see that?"

He came to the window. "That glow?"

"What is that?" She leaned closer to the

pane. The glow grew by the barn, joined by another. The forms filled out, growing limbs. "Am I crazy, or do those look like…?"

"Ghosts." Nolan wrapped his hand around her waist and pulled her against him. Two ghosts turned into three, which turned into six. Soon, more than two dozen figures drifted over the lawn. Their features were undetectable, but the shapes of their bodies formed the unmistakable outlines of people.

"Dante," Lily called, "Polly?"

"Ow, damn gnomes! Who keeps putting you…" Dante swore from the hallway a few times before his voice trailed off completely.

"Who invited guests?" Polly appeared in light blue pajamas with pink bunny slippers. Her bright red hair was wrapped with a sheer pink scarf. "Oh dear, sugar bee, they're not very happy. Did you summon them from the bad place?"

"I didn't summon anyone," Lily protested. "I drank water."

"Oo, I like it, wolf-boy, very breezy. The hospital gave us your belongings, but I like this outfit much better." Polly nodded at Nolan's hospital gown in approval. Nolan grabbed the back of his gown and held it together while turning his back to the counter. "Finally someone around here with a little fashion courage." Then, lowering her voice, she winked and said, "Nice bum."

"Polly, please, I need you to focus. How do we keep ghosts out? Or better yet, send them away?"

"I'll get the salt," Polly said.

"Yes, salt circles to keep ghosts out. I remember hearing about that somewhere." Lily nodded.

"No, for margaritas. You look like you could use a drink to relax. You're too tense. I blame Mara. She has a spotted aura."

"Mara." Lily couldn't believe she'd forgotten all about the woman. "Is she still around? Did she come back? Is she all right?"

"The hitchhiker you picked up? No, Polly said she ran out of here." Dante joined them.

"She wasn't a hitchhiker," Lily clarified.

"Florus and I cleansed the house while you were out," Polly added. "And put up a few protection spells."

"Is that what you were doing? I thought you were decorating." Dante narrowed his gaze and walked toward the window. "Are any of you seeing this?"

The ghosts had drifted to stand on the lawn, looking at the house. Well, to be honest, she couldn't tell if they were looking or facing away, but either way they were creepy.

"Polly, can't you do something to get rid of them?" Lily asked. The woman didn't answer. When she turned around, Polly was gone. "Polly?" She hurried to the dining room. "Polly?" She tried the living room and library before running to the stairs. "Polly, where did you go?" She circled back to the kitchen. "I think she ran aw—"

Dante and Nolan were gone too.

"Away," she whispered.

Thump. Thump. Thump.

A steady knock sounded on the back door. She shivered, going toward the noise. She stood several feet back as she peered through the storm door. A transparent figure looked in at her, the features more filled out than those of the specters on the lawn. Color filled in the ghost's translucent features. Long dark hair fell over her shoulders. A floral dress cinched tightly to her waist and flared at her hips.

"Nolan? Help?" Lily whispered, unable to make her voice any louder.

Thump. Thump. Thump.

The knock sounded again, but the ghost woman didn't move. Lily stared at her, willing her to go away, watching for the moment she'd float through the door and come inside. Her heart beat fast and hard and she found it difficult to breathe. This ghost was not like Stan the miner. This one didn't speak, didn't laugh.

Thump. Thump. Thump.

"This isn't happening." Lily shivered as a chill washed over her body.

Thump. Thump. Thump.

"Aunt Polly?"

Thump. Thump. Thump.

"Dante? Come on, Dante, where are you?"

Thump. Thump. Thump.

Thump. Thump. Thump.

"Stop it," Lily ordered

Thump. Thump. Thump.

"Nolan, please, where are you?" she begged.

Thump. Thump. Thump.

"Fine, hello, hi, how can I help you?" Lily yelled at the door. "What do you want? No, you can't come inside. We're not buying. No solicitors."

She waited, but the knocking stopped.

"Hello?" she repeated. Why was the ghost just staring at her? Why wasn't she moving?

"Do ya know one of yer guests has one of them fancy dinners swimming around in their room? Want me to fish it out of there so we can fry it up?"

Lily spun to where Stan sat on the kitchen counter. His thumbs were hooked in his waistband. He kicked his feet. His heels dipped through the doors of the bottom cabinets.

"What do they want?" Lily motioned toward the yard.

"Who?" Stan leaned over to look. "Ah, yeah, the floaters. Wonder what they're doing here. Normally they don't leave town."

Thump. Thump. Thump.

"Oh, quiet." Stan waved his arm at the woman ghost at the door. "No one is letting you in to leak ectoplasm all over the place."

Thump. Thump. Thump.

Stan leapt off the counter and began thrusting his hips side to side in a strange rhythm as he sang, "Thud and a thump. Thud, rump, bump. Thump, bump, hump. Thumpity, thump, thump." His song ended with a knee slap.

Thump!

The woman ghost gave one last knock before she disappeared from the doorway.

"I can't believe that worked. She's gone. How did that work?" Lily looked out the back door, leaning from side to side to get a wider view. The glowing figures of light still stood on the lawn.

The black cat jumped in front of the window and she jerked back.

"Ee-hee-hee-hee." Stan's laugh was mocking. "Ya should see yer face."

"What do they want?" Lily ignored the spirit's merriment.

"To suck yer life from yer veins," Stan said.

Lily grabbed her neck in fright.

Stan's laughter rang out over the kitchen, grating against her nerves. "What do you *think* they want? They're floaters. You invited them over and they float. Sally's a knocker. Always with the thump, thud, thump. She wanders door to door, knocking and waiting. No one ever lets her in."

"I didn't invite them."

"Someone called them."

"Can you make them leave?" Lily wasn't sure how she felt about Stan being her ally in this situation, but considering everyone else had disappeared on her, she wasn't given much of a choice.

"Tell me about that feisty redhead walking around the place. She's a whole crate of dynamite. Boom!" Stan's beard hairs shifted as he grinned. "She got a man?"

"Polly?" Lily shrugged. "I don't know. She never said."

"Yeah, she's got a man. The fiery ones always

do." Stan sighed longingly, even as he smiled. "Moths to a flame. Dynamite."

"Boom," Lily muttered, watching the lawn.

"Yeah, boom." Stan nodded.

"Stan, do—?" Lily looked at the counter to see he was gone. She was alone. Feeling a hand on her cheek, Lily let that someone turned her head. The world shifted, and she was staring at Nolan. The hard kitchen floor was beneath her back.

"The ghosts are gone," Dante said.

"She's back," Nolan answered. "Lily? How do you feel? You fainted."

"No, *you* disappeared." When she tried to push up from the floor, she felt dizzy and had to lie back down.

"Take it easy. I think you're overheated." Nolan's concerned gaze examined her.

"Margaritas!" Polly entered holding a pitcher. She leaned over to look at Lily. "What are you doing down there?"

"Talking to dead people," Lily answered.

"Oh." Polly nodded as if it made complete sense. "Very well then. Margarita?"

"Yes," Lily said.

"No," Nolan answered for her at the same time.

"Open wide." Polly made a motion like she

was going to pour the margarita into Lily's mouth directly from the pitcher.

"I'll get up." This time she fought the dizziness as she sat upright.

"Suit yourself." Polly pointed at Dante. "Florus, get cups."

"My name is Dante," he muttered, as he did what he was told. He placed mismatched glasses on the counter.

"That's not what your birth certificate says," Lily teased.

"Stop it," Nolan demanded, a little loudly. They all turned to look at him in surprise. "What's wrong with you people? Not everything is a joke. Someone has threatened you. They've burnt your lawn, spray-painted your house, knocked down your barn, and not to mention the ghosts surrounding the house and driving my truck off a cliff—a truck Lily could have been in. You're infested with gnomes and have a rabid raccoon coughing up magic hairballs. And—"

Lily placed her hand on Nolan's mouth, quieting him with her fingers. His firm lips were warm against her skin. "We know all that, and I promise you, we take it seriously."

Nolan pulled at her wrist, drawing her fingers from his mouth. "It's too dangerous here. I think you should consider leaving Lucky Valley."

"It's dangerous everywhere," Lily answered. "This is our home. We won't be pushed out of it."

"No inheritance is worth your life," he insisted.

Lily stared at him, remembering the kiss. Her eyes moved to his mouth. His concern was touching, but unnecessary. She wasn't running away.

"Are you two going to make out or something? Because I don't need to be emotionally scarred," Dante said.

"Shut up, Dante," Lily answered, though she did lean back a little from Nolan. She resisted the urge to kiss him. Then to Nolan, she said, "Stan scared Sally away. She's the knocking ghost. He said we should never invite her in. The ghosts on the lawn are floaters. It sounds like they're harmless."

"When did you talk to Stan?" Dante asked.

"You say I fainted. I say you all disappeared, and I had a conversation with a ghost." Lily stood and took a glass from Polly. "Now, I'm exhausted." She took a long drink, thankful for the strength of the liquor in Polly's concoction. Handing an empty glass back to her aunt, she said, "Stan has a crush on you. He wants to know if you have a man."

"Captain Petey?" Polly asked in surprise.

"Oh, I've seen our future, and we're meant to always be close friends, but *just* friends."

"Okay." Though curious, Lily didn't want to start a long conversation and she had a feeling that would be a big one. "Stan also wants to eat Herman. I'm going to bed."

Chapter Sixteen

"You know we laugh and joke because it's easier than crying."

Nolan opened his eyes, coming out of a deep sleep. He was naked under the covers, having crawled in after taking a quick shower. His leg throbbed angrily from the puncture wounds and subsequent hike.

Lily stood at the end of the bed, watching him.

"Good, you're alive. It's past noon, and I just came out of my sleep coma, too. I think Polly's margaritas had more than liquor in them." Lily's hair was pulled into a messy bun on the top of her head. Her sleeveless blue t-shirt and jeans made it look like she was ready to work.

"Magical margaritas." Nolan chuckled. He wouldn't be surprised if that was the case. Polly had ushered him off to bed soon after he drank one. He remembered starting to nod off in the shower. "Have you been standing there long?"

"Watching you sleep? Only about fifteen minutes," she said. He arched a brow. Lily laughed. "See, jokes, we Goodes are funny people. No, I knocked and when you didn't answer, I became worried. How's your back?"

"Doesn't hurt," he lied. "How's your magic?"

"Still misfiring. I hiccupped and set the kitchen curtains on fire. Luckily, Dante was able to put them out before any real damage was done." Lily turned her back when he sat up. The covers slid from his chest to his waist. "Polly was telling me that the Crawford side is all potions, spells, and natural elemental magic. The Goode side is a little more fireballs and teleportation." Lily sighed. "So before I teleport myself into a wall, or set the entire place on fire, I thought it might help to expend my energy doing something a little more productive while I wait for the bad luck to dissipate."

"Like?"

"Salvaging any of the old barn wood I can for resale. I doubt we can rebuild with the old lumber, but we shouldn't let it go to waste. Besides, unless someone in town would be willing to hire me, I need to make money somehow." She looked at her hands, her back still to him as she leaned against the foot of the bed.

"I thought you had the trust," he said.

"It covers the structures only. We can't buy food with it, and I can't keep relying on Polly every time I want to eat. We can't buy clothes or new phones... oh, hey, check it out." She pulled a small gray flip phone out of her pocket. "Look at the high-tech hardware that was delivered this morning. I have a phone again."

There was something intimate about having her in his room. The memory of their kiss remained on his lips. He didn't regret it, but she hadn't mentioned it again, and so neither did he. Maybe he was foolish for thinking a powerful Goode witch could be interested in a werewolf like him.

Nolan swung his feet to the floor and laid the covers across his midsection. "There's a guy in town, Garrett, who makes furniture. He owns Nail in the Coffin Carpentry. I can give him a call and see if he wants to take some of it off your hands."

He was sure not too many locals would want

a piece of Goode property in their homes or businesses, but he'd sure as heck try to sell it for her.

"That sounds like a morbid name for a business," she said.

"His ancestors were the undertakers in Unlucky Valley." He glanced around his room. When he stood, he took the sheets with him and tucked them around his waist. "Toss me a shirt from my bag?"

As she moved to his duffle bag, she said, "You can use the dresser. You're here all the time now anyway."

Nolan couldn't help but laugh. "Is that a hint?"

"Yes." She threw the shirt in his direction without looking and he leaned over to catch it. "I'm hinting that I want my own bathroom with its own hot water tank. I've decided I don't like sharing hot water with everyone in the house, and it's just going to become worse when we start having guests."

"You still want to have the bed and breakfast after all that's been going on around here?" Nolan slid the shirt over his head, wearing the sheet like a lavalava.

"Why not? Haunted destinations are all the rage, and I won't have to pay people to fake weird things happening." Her head turned to the side, but she kept her back to him. "The trust ensures the house and land will always be taken care of and remain in the family, but whoever set it up forgot to take care of the people living in the house." She reached for the duffle bag and tossed it on the bed within his reach. "So, I'm creating my own loophole. Let the family trust take care of the remodeling and any damage done by guests. Let it pay the utility bills and the property taxes. The money we make will go toward groceries, and clothes, and a new car—nothing fancy—and eventually we'll add Unlucky Valley ghost tours and history tours, and maybe build a series of cabins for those who want privacy and—"

"Whoa, Lily, take a breath." Nolan finished getting dressed.

"I can't explain it. I woke up today and everything is clear. First we get this house ready for guests. Then we form an LLC, hire some people, put up a website—"

"Don't you think you need to be having this conversation with your brother?"

"Why?" This time she did turn.

"Because you're planning a business with him."

"Oh, no, I'm sorry, I forgot an important part

of my plan." She came toward him. "I'm going to need help. I love Dante, but I know him. Running a bed and breakfast is not his style. He'll hang out for a while but then disappear when something else comes along. My sister, Jesse, isn't ready for that kind of responsibility, and she's refusing to even visit. Aunt Polly," Lily pursed her lips and sighed heavily as she shook her head, "enough said."

"So…?"

"Oh, sorry. *You.* I want you to be my partner. You know about broken heaters and pipes and wallpaper-y things."

"Wallpaper-y things?"

"Yes." Lily nodded. "If our work here—what little work we've managed to get done between hauntings and raccoon attacks—tells me anything, it's that I know nothing about wallpaper-y things. I need a partner who does. You've said more than once that the city inspector gig is not really your thing, so I thought, if you were interested, we could form a partnership."

Partnership. It wasn't exactly the offer he wanted from her.

"Are you hesitating because of the kiss?" Her eyes dipped to his mouth, but she leaned back.

"We should probably discuss it."

"Okay." She looked at him expectantly.

Nolan wasn't sure what he was supposed to say. Did he tell her the truth? Did he tell her he thought about kissing her often? Did he tell her he wanted more than that? Did he tell her how he felt?

He finally decided on, "Maybe we shouldn't discuss it."

"Okay. If that's what you want, we'll pretend it never happened." Lily's eyes moved away from his. He studied her expression. Her smile fell. "What about the partnership? Did I mention it would be fifty-fifty?"

"No." Nolan touched her arm, causing her eyes to meet his again. "I think sixty-forty."

"You want sixty?" Her eyes widened in surprise.

"I want forty. This is your property, your house, your idea. You should have the majority. I wouldn't feel right taking half." He dropped his hand from her arm, even as he wanted to pull her closer.

"No. We're looking at a lot of work. I'd need you to take care of the grounds and the maintenance. Fifty-fifty."

"Sixty-forty."

"Fifty-one and forty-nine." She crossed her arms over her chest. "Final offer."

"Deal." Nolan held out his hand. "Partner."

"Really?" Her smile returned. When he nodded, she clapped her hands a couple of times in excitement before grasping his hand. "Yay!"

Her hand remained on his. Fear tried to creep into the happy moment. He knew he had to protect her. As soon as he could slip away, he was going to have a conversation with the town council to see who else they'd tasked with running the Goodes out of town so he could put a stop to it.

"You get started on a plan for," she waved her hand around to encompass the house, "all of the construction stuff, and I'll get working on a business plan so the lawyer can draw up contracts for us." She let go and hurried toward the door. "I can't believe we're going to make Garden Gnome Bed and Breakfast a reality."

Nolan started to laugh at her enthusiasm, but stopped as the name sunk in. "Wait, what?" He rushed after her. "I can't own something called Garden Gnome Bed and Breakfast. Can't we call it The Goode Estate? Lucky Valley Hotel? Were-wolf Inn? Something more... *manly?*"

He heard her footsteps moving down the stairs and tripped on a gnome standing outside his door. The round-cheeked statue stared up at Nolan as he rocked on his back. Nolan picked the gnome up and placed him next to the wall.

He patted the statue on the pointy hat. "Sorry, buddy."

"If you hurt her, I'll set your hairy butt on fire." Dante stood up from the stairwell leading to the third floor. He'd been sitting on the bottom step in the shadows.

"It was only a kiss," Nolan said. "I would never hurt her."

Dante arched a brow. "Kiss? I was talking about Lily's business idea. She needs it to work. We no longer have jobs waiting for us in Washington and the funds are getting pretty low."

Just how bad was Lily's financial situation? It never occurred to him that a Goode might need financial assistance.

"Oh, ah, yeah, don't worry. I won't do anything to hurt the business. I think it's a great idea, if we can get the spirits and gnomes to behave." Nolan didn't relish the idea of arguing with a witch who'd just received his powers.

"Wait." Dante approached, tilting his head to study Nolan's face. "You kissed my sister, and she didn't deck you?"

"I think that's something you should talk to your sister about." He might have let it slip, but Nolan was not about to kiss and tell.

"Wow. She must really like you, wolf boy. Maybe I was wrong. Maybe she could be interested in you." Dante slapped him on the arm. "Good luck with that. Better men than you have tried to crack through that armor. Don't say I didn't warn you."

Chapter Seventeen

"Are you sure this is a good idea?" Lily took hold of Nolan's arm, keeping him from walking into Stammerin' Eddie's. "The last time I was in town they chased me up a tree."

"Two teenagers chased you up a tree. These are adults." Nolan peered in the diner's window. "Wait, no, I see what you mean. Five-year-old June Martin can be scary."

"Are you making fun of me?" Lily hit Nolan's arm playfully.

He pretended to shield himself. "Only a little."

"This is Lucky Valley, so it's possible those brown ringlets transform into snakes and she turns people into stone." Lily tried to keep walking.

"Oh, please, we haven't had a Medusa in town for decades." He blocked her from fleeing. "If you want a business here, you need to make friends with the locals. Luckily, there—"

"No, don't talk about luck."

"Luckily," he repeated, "there have been no more fires started on the lawn. Maybe they were just pranks and whoever did it grew bored when they didn't get a bigger reaction out of you."

"What if I bring my bad luck in there with me and make things worse?" Lily tried to keep walking, but he looped his arm into hers and swung her toward the glass door. If she tried to leave now, it would be obvious as there were people looking at her. Under her breath, she muttered, "I kind of don't like you right now."

"I'm sorry to hear that. I like you very much." Nolan pushed open the door and stepped close to her back to force her inside.

"Nolan," the woman behind the counter greeted. Her auburn hair was pulled back, and she wore black, rectangular, plastic glasses. The red polo shirt with the business logo held a nametag that read "Sal" in bold letters. Her eyes went to Lily, clearly seeing she had two customers, but she didn't acknowledge the second. "Pick a booth, I'll be right back."

The front counter barstools were full of

customers drinking coffee. A few of them eyed her as she walked past. She tried to smile, but that only seemed to make it worse, as their expressions became suspicious. The rectangular seating area, beyond the food prep station and stools, was long and skinny. Black-and-white tiles checkered the floor, and shiny silver lined the ceiling. Behind the counter, old-fashioned soda fountains, a soft serve machine, blenders, and the largest coffee maker she'd ever seen spread along the back wall. A serving window glowed red with heat lamps.

The low murmur of noise from patrons died down until stopping altogether. Red booths lined both sides of the diner, creating a walkway through the middle. Tin signs of 1950s food logos graced the walls. Of course, the only open table was near the back, so they were forced down the aisle lined with watchful eyes.

"Been awhile since we've seen you here for supper, Nolan," said a bearded man, one amongst a table of many. The five men looked like a plainclothes Santa convention with varying depths of graying beards. Only there was nothing jolly about their expressions. They looked at her like she'd ruined Christmas.

"Gentlemen," Nolan greeted the men. "How've you been?"

Grunts and small, disapproving moans answered him.

"Fish haven't been biting," the first bearded man muttered with a side-eye glance at Lily.

"I had three flat tires," Santa number three added.

"Mm-hmm," Santa four agreed. "He did. Three different times."

"My niece set her kitchen of fire," number five said. "I have to build her all new cabinets."

Lily automatically looked at Santa number two, to see what his complaint would be. He merely lifted a bandaged hand that appeared to be missing a forefinger.

Lily had the insane urge to apologize, even as she knew none of it had been her doing. Before she could speak, Nolan ended the conversation. "Good seeing you, gentleman, we'll let you get back to your meal."

She tried to hurry to the empty table and managed to pass two more booths before June Martin's father tucked her under his arm in a protective gesture. A redhead ducked behind a menu as if the laminated trifold could protect her. Conversely, the dark-haired man she was with didn't stop staring.

"Maybe we should order to go," Lily said softly to Nolan.

"Maybe she should take it and move out of town," someone whispered a little too loudly.

Lily's gaze darted to a middle-aged woman in a paisley dress.

Nolan pretended not to hear the rude comment. "I know you want to get back to work on the help wanted ads, but you need to eat. This new business is not going to get off the ground if you don't take care of yourself."

He spoke loud enough for everyone to hear him but looked at her as if they had a private conversation. He led her to the empty booth, and she slid onto the red cushioned seat.

"Nolan—"

He cut her off by handing her one of the menus stored against the wall behind the salt and pepper shakers. "Eat first, business plan later."

She leaned forward and whispered, "What are you talking about?"

He looked at his menu. "Wait for it."

Sal appeared at the table with an order pad. "Haven't seen you here in a while. We were about to send a search and rescue team out to save…" She glanced at Lily, and it was clear she amended what she'd been about to say. "Out to your house."

"Hey, Sally. Yeah, I took a second job at the Goode Estate and they've been feeding me pretty well." Nolan smiled at the waitress before turning back to his menu.

Sal looked at him like he'd just announced he was growing a second head.

"Don't you have that memorized by now?" Another woman joined Sal. She was older but wore the same red uniform with the nametag "Edna" on her shirt. Her short black hair was curled around the top of her head but cropped short by the ears and neck.

"How are you doing, darlin'?" Nolan stood and gave the woman a hug. Lily arched a brow at the way his tone changed.

"Now, you stop that, Mr. Nolan Dawson. You know my Eddie is the jealous type." Edna swatted his hand, but the smile never left her face.

Sal backed away, waited for a few seconds, and then went to check on her other tables. Lily was aware of the surrounding quiet as everyone tried not to stare at them.

"Who's your friend?" Edna's was the first genuinely kind smile she'd seen from the Lucky Valley townsfolk. As Nolan introduced her, Lily waited for that expression to change.

"I would like you to meet Lily Goode. She has some big plans for the Goode Estate." Nolan slid back into his seat across from her.

"*We* have big plans," Lily amended.

"She has me doing construction," Nolan said.

"I heard somewhere you were looking for help? What kind of help? People always need jobs," Edna said. "Maybe I can send them your way. Everyone comes in here eventually."

Lily glanced at Nolan, who merely grinned. Since walking through the diner was the first time hiring people had been mentioned outside the house, it was pretty easy to figure out when Edna had heard the rumor.

"Lily's going to open up a bed and breakfast—"

"*We*," Lily inserted.

"—and try to bring tourism to the area. She has big plans," Nolan said. "Can I get a coffee, chocolate milk shake, and a Big Eddie burger?"

"Sure thing, hon, you want fries?" Edna asked.

"Always," he said.

"And for you?" Edna turned to Lily, not writing the order down.

"Coffee, vanilla shake, and the Stammerin' Sandwich with fries." Lily put the menu back by the wall.

"You don't want that," Edna said.

"Oh, ah…?" Lily looked at the menu but didn't pick it back up.

"Trust me, Eddie bought a new hot pepper sauce and it will set your mouth on fire. Everyone is staying away from that sandwich." Edna shook her head. "It will strip the paint off a car." She gestured toward the Santa table, leaned forward, covered her mouth and said, "How do you think Stanley lost his finger?"

Lily paused, unsure if it was polite to laugh.

Edna waved her hand in the air. "That last one was a joke, dear. How about you let me make you something special?"

Nolan's eyes widened, and he shook his head slightly in denial. But Edna was looking at her expectantly, and she was being so friendly, that Lily found herself saying, "That would be great, thank you, Edna."

Edna nodded. "Be right back with the coffees."

"Edna will spread the word," Nolan said.

"I hope it's a good word." Lily tried to slide down in her seat a little to hide from the prying eyes.

"It will be. She likes you." Nolan rested his arms on the table.

"How can you tell?" Lily kept low in her seat without trying to be obvious.

"She didn't let you eat the tongue-melting sandwich."

Sal returned with the coffee cups and a small bowl of creamers before leaving again. The waitress didn't say a word.

Lily lifted the cup and sniffed. "I really hope this is better than last time."

"Best coffee on the planet," Nolan assured her.

"Apparently you don't remember what the Goode-Crawford curse did to the coffee machine." Lily dared a sip, bracing herself for something horrible, and was pleasantly surprised. She sat up straighter and took another sip of the hot liquid and nodded her head. "Oh, wow, that is a really good cup of coffee."

"Maybe luck is turning around." Nolan barely got the words out before a loud pop sounded behind the counter.

Almost everyone in the place jumped in their seats.

Lily lifted up in her seat to see Sal standing behind the counter, covered in the vanilla shake. The blender looked as if the top had exploded off of it, sending ice cream and milk flying. Liquid dripped down the walls and off the metal counter. The blender made a horrible grinding noise as if stuck.

Rrrr, rrrr, rrrr, rrrr…

It was the only sound in the silent diner.

"Oh, come on," Lily grumbled under her breath. "I didn't do that."

Had she?

As if on cue, Sal and the patrons turned to look accusingly in her direction.

Sal flicked her hands, picked up the chocolate milk shake, and walked toward Lily and Nolan. She placed the chocolate in front of Nolan, saying, "I'm sorry. The milk shake blender stopped working. I'm not able to get you your vanilla shake."

Sal dripped vanilla on the table. The waitress walked away, leaving everyone to stare at Lily as if she'd singlehandedly destroyed all ice cream production in the state.

Nolan unwrapped his silverware from the napkin and cleaned the droplets. "Just smile and keep talking to me."

"That's easy for you to say. Your back is turned to everyone and they're not staring at you." Lily kept her eyes on the table.

"Easy to fix." Nolan slid out of the booth, only to join her on her side. He pulled his milk-shake in front of them and then rested his arm behind her. He leaned his face close to her ear. It was an intimate gesture and not missed by the others in the diner. So only she could hear, he said against her cheek, "We'll give them something else to gossip about."

"They'll probably think I put a spell on you and hate me more." She touched the thick stem of the milkshake glass and adjusted it needlessly on the table before resting her hand on her lap.

"Well, I am a catch," Nolan teased. She punched his thigh under the table. "You want some of my shake? I'll share."

"Edna's special pick for me will probably be a poison pellet sandwich." Lily liked his nearness and drew comfort from it.

"Try not to think of it as against you. Remember that to them, you're an outsider coming into a town full of secrets. This town is distrustful of others by nature. They have to be. They need time to see you're not going to hurt them, or expose them, or curse them. They need to give you a chance." He slipped his hand over hers and let it rest on her leg. "And you need to give them a chance. The way you think they're looking at you, you're looking at them just as suspiciously."

Lily took a deep breath and nodded. "You're right. This is not a normal situation. I'm a witch and they're all... What are they, exactly?"

"There is an unspoken rule that we don't expose each other's secrets." Nolan traced her fingers. "I will tell you there is a fairy, a bennu, a minotaur descendent, a werewolf, and an Erinyes."

"Fairy is the redhead who keeps trying to pretend she's not looking at us. She seems delicate and flighty. The minotaur is the young man she's with. He has a bullish personality. And he's going on my potential-suspects-for-vandalizing-the-house list. He's got that angry look in his eyes." She reached over and tapped his thigh. "Werewolf." Then withdrew her hand. "I have no clue what a bennu or an Erinyes are."

"Flighty and bullish? You don't think your presumptions are a little bit stereotypical?"

"Am I wrong?" she met his gaze and was captured by it. He was close, and even if she didn't consciously let herself think of it, her lips remembered the feel of his.

"No. You're not wrong." His didn't look away, and she felt him leaning closer.

"Well, looks like there's more than construction going on at the old Goode Estate," Edna interrupted. Lily hadn't even heard the woman approach. She slid a plate in front of Nolan, "One Big Eddie, and one grilled cheese."

"Oh, thanks." Lily looked at the plain sandwich. It wasn't exactly what she would have ordered.

"I'll be back with the rest." Edna left.

"The rest?" Lily asked Nolan.

"Wait for it." He turned his plate to reangle his food and grabbed his sandwich.

Edna came back with a burger, chili-and-cheese nachos, a bowl of chili, broccoli-and-cheese soup, chicken sandwich, and three kinds of pie. "There you are. Enjoy!"

"Uh…" Lily looked to Nolan for help. "Why does everyone keep trying to feed me? First Polly and now Edna. Do I look like I'm starving?"

"Edna always tries to overfeed everyone. If you let her pick, you're going to get a lot of options." He gestured at the chili. "You going to eat that?"

Lily chuckled and slid the bowl toward him. "Take it. Please help."

She picked up a triangle of grilled cheese and dipped it in the broccoli soup. As she leaned over to take a bite, her phone rang. Chewing, she dropped the food, wiped her hands on a napkin and pulled the cheap phone out of her pocket to answer. She smiled at Nolan and made a show of flipping it open to answer the call. It really was the least expensive phone she could find. It made calls, it received calls, and texting by numerical keypad took hours. "Hey, Dante, what's up?"

"Are you safe?" Her brother's panic was palpable. "Where are you?"

"Uh, why? I'm at the diner downtown. What's happening?"

"What is it?" Nolan asked. She held up her hand to silence him so she could hear her brother.

"There's been another attack on the…" The sound of sirens drowned out Dante's voice. She plugged her opposite ear and leaned closer to the window in an effort to hear him better. "I—"

A thud sounded, and then there were only sirens.

Her eyes widened and she tried to stand, but Nolan was blocking her way out of the booth. She tapped his arm frantically. "We have to go. Something's wrong."

He instantly stood, reached for his wallet, and threw cash on the table. "Let's go."

"Dante? I can't hear you?" Lily followed Nolan as she tried to hear her brother. She didn't care what the patrons thought of her hasty departure. "Dante? Dante!"

Chapter Eighteen

The orange glow on the horizon that emanated from the spot where the Victorian should be caused Nolan to press down on the gas pedal of Lily's car as he sped toward it. Black smoke slithered into the sky, signaling the danger ahead. Lily pressed her hand into the dashboard, bracing herself as they took a corner too fast and the tires slid on the dirt road.

"Please, please, please," she pleaded under her breath.

There was nothing he could say to comfort her.

"Fire." Lily gripped his arm as a firetruck came into view. Orange flames consumed the back of the house. "Oh, no, Dante, please don't be in there. Please, please, please..."

Nolan felt her fear rippling over him. He hit the brakes, slowing so he could turn up the drive. Deputy Herczeg's truck blocked the way, and he skidded to avoid hitting it. Lily jumped out before they had come to a complete stop.

Nolan raced after her as she made her way across the front lawn. She leapt over a random garden gnome sitting cross-legged in the yard, and then the firehose coming from the pumper truck. When he caught up to her, she was nearing the fire.

He grabbed her arm, jerking her back. "Lily, watch out."

A hard stream of water shot out from behind the house. She would have run right into it.

A fireman stepped into view. Nolan knew the entire crew. They were good people, and all had supernatural gifts related to the water. Captain Santos manned the hose at the nozzle. He had the strength of three men and didn't need help directing the stream. There was a running joke in town about his bushy mustache being a thing of great beauty. Only a few men could pull off such a specimen, but as an ipupiara, he seemed to have a face made for it.

Three others—Kelly, Walsh, and Murphy— were finfolk. They could transform into three forms—fish, human, or a hybrid of the two. The

226

last firefighter, Agnes, was a naiad, a rare kind of water spirit. She couldn't be away from fresh water for longer than a few hours, so riding around on a pumper truck was a perfect job for her.

The pile of barn wood blazed, feeding a giant bonfire that did not look close to being under control. Scorched siding dripped with water on the back of the house. There was damage, but the structure was intact.

"Lily, look, the house is fine. I'm sure Dante and Polly are—"

"Polly!" Her cry cut him off. She tugged on his arm as if to command him to follow. Because of the firefighters blocking the way through the backyard, they had to run the long way around the house to reach Polly. "What happened? Where's Dante?"

"I don't know what happened, sugar bee," Polly said, watching the flames. "This shouldn't have occurred. Everything is topsy-turvy. There's a force I can't predict. We had no warning it was coming."

"Polly, please." Lily grabbed her aunt's arms and made her look at her. "Where's my brother?"

"Here. I'm here." Dante came from beside the house. She hadn't seen him on her way around and guessed his stupid ass must have been inside.

Lily threw her arms around his neck. "Where were you? Why the hell did you hang up on me? I was terrified. What happened? What if...?" She motioned to the flames. "I thought you were..."

"Get back," Lieutenant Kelly ordered. He waved them away from the fire.

"The chick fireman bumped me, and my phone went flying." Dante pointed to the barn. "I couldn't get to it. I'm pretty sure it's ruined. It was good while it lasted. I guess I just have to share your phone now."

"Don't say chick fireman." Lily hit her brother's arm. "They're firefighters."

"I said get back," Kelly commanded.

Nolan lifted his arm to urge them away from the flames. He scanned the ground, seeing clear evidence of a burn pattern leading from the barn and the back of the house. This fire wasn't an accident. His eyes shifted, and he focused past the blaze. He detected movement in the trees, but it was too far to make out who or what watched them. The roar of fire and water created a white noise that made it hard to hear past. Firefighters called commands to each other.

"Good, you're all accounted for." Deputy Herczeg held a small notepad as she stopped next to them. "You'll have to wait until they clear the house before you can go inside." She pulled a pen out of her front breast pocket. "Any idea who would want to burn down your house?"

"Maybe the same person who burnt our lawn, or spray-painted the siding, or knocked down the barn," Lily said. "Maybe if you had taken our report seriously the first time instead of dismissing it, we wouldn't be here."

Herczeg slapped her pen down on the pad without writing anything down.

"We don't know," Dante amended for his sister. "It could have been the ghosts that showed up on the lawn, or—"

"Dante." Lily tried to shush her brother.

"Don't look at me like that," Dante dismissed his sister. "It's Lucky Valley. Like ghosts are a big secret. You're dating a werewolf."

Nolan looked at Lily to see her reaction. Her eyes met his, but she didn't protest the comment.

"That fireman—sorry, *firefighter*—has scales," Dante continued. "We're witches. Polly tried to set me up on a date with a troll."

"She's a lovely girl," Polly interrupted.

"What's wrong with trolls?" Herczeg asked. She put her pen back in her pocket.

Dante had the good sense, for once, not to open his smart-alecky mouth.

"So I was right. This is a Goode problem, not a police problem," Herczeg concluded. "I have no jurisdiction over ghosts. Only those supernaturals who have permanent corporeal form."

"It might not be ghosts. It could be…" Lily hesitated and looked around. Seeing a gnome, she pointed at the pointy-hatted suspect. "It could be gnomes."

"What?" Polly gasped. "The gnomes are our friends. They protect."

"They appear all over the house like creepy little voyeurs," Dante said.

"Quiet, Florus," Polly scolded, "or no cupcakes for you."

"And plastic pink flamingos helped by spray painting your house?" Herczeg arched a brow. "You do know they're lawn ornaments, right?"

"It's not the gnomes," Polly insisted. "And flamingos can't spray. They don't have hands."

"I'll talk to the sheriff about checking the surrounding woods," the deputy said. "Until we hire more help, there are only two of us. We'll do the best we can."

"Ask some of the shifters," Nolan suggested. "We can run the entire area in a few hours."

Herczeg checked her watch and then shook her head. "No. We're not going to do that."

"Why not?" Lily asked. "Do you think it's too

dangerous? Nolan, I don't want you putting your-self in danger. Maybe you should let the police handle it."

The deputy gave Nolan a meaningful look and glanced up at the sky. How could he have forgotten what tonight was?

"She's right. We can't do it now. We'll do it tomorrow." Nolan turned to watch the flames. He'd known the wolf inside him for so long, that he'd not even thought about the tingling in his limbs, the warning that always came before the full moon.

He took Lily's hand and pulled her away from the others. The orange firelight danced on her features. He wanted to protect her, more than anything. This threat wasn't a prank, couldn't be shrugged off or explained away. It wasn't ghosts, or gnomes. It was serious. And he couldn't stay to protect her.

"What is it?" Lily reached to touch his arm.

"I have to leave." He looked at the fire, the muddy ground, anywhere but at her face.

"What? Now? With this?" She stepped between him and the fire, forcing him to look at her. "Nolan, you can't go. I…" Her voice dropped. "I need you."

"You need me?" The words gave him great pleasure.

"I need your help." Her eyes begged him. "Please stay."

"Get your brother and Polly and go book a room in town for the night." Nolan turned as he heard a shout. A beam collapsed into the pile. Flames arced. "Make sure you lock your doors."

"I feel like there's something you're not telling me again." Her words were drowned out by several shouts and the rush of water from the hose as Santos stepped closer to them.

"It's a full moon," he tried to explain.

"Go, go, go," Santos shouted.

"What?" she yelled over the noise.

"Left," Kelly ordered.

"No, right," Walsh countered.

"I can't come because it's a full moon," he said louder.

She plugged her ear facing the fire and yelled louder. "What?"

"It's jumping to the house," Santos said. "Get in front of it."

"Nolan, now!" the deputy ordered.

"What?" she repeated before lifting her hands in irritation. She gestured at the fire, crying, "Just put the damn fire out already!"

A loud *whoosh* of air rose around the barn. People stumbled for footing. Their hair blew toward the flames. The fire turned almost instantly into a mushroom cloud of dark smoke. The water stream continued to fly from the hose onto the smoking boards for a few more seconds before Santos closed the nozzle.

Silence was punctured by dripping water. Movement seemed to happen in slow motion as the firefighters stopped working. Lily's hands shook as they remained lifted toward the barn. Her stunned expression remained frozen.

"Lily." Nolan took her hands in his.

"My sugar bee is a fully baked little cookie," Polly exclaimed.

"Did I…?" Lily looked at him helplessly.

Her hands seemed to buzz with energy in his.

"That was awesome, Lily," Dante said. "So much cooler than levitating a chair."

"Let's pack it up," Santos ordered, his voice not as gruff as before.

"Nolan, let's move," Herczeg said.

Nolan looked up at the sky. "I have to go. I'm sorry."

She gripped him tighter.

"Nolan, do you have a trap here?" the deputy asked.

"No." He shook his head.

"I'll give you a ride to your house. Let's go." Herczeg didn't wait for him to agree.

Nolan wished he could explain more about

the Dawson curse, but was only able to say, "full moon," before running after the deputy. It may already be too late, but at least the deputy would know how to stop him if he turned before making it to his chains.

Chapter Nineteen

Lily watched everyone moving around her as if in slow motion. Nothing inside her made sense. She was hot and cold, shaky and steady, fatigued and energized.

As the power had exploded out of her body, the world around her became clear. Firefighters hauled their equipment, motioning at each other. Dante watched the action, his hands on his hips. Nolan disappeared around the side of the house. Polly did a bizarre jig as she danced in a circle, her elbows flapping up like an excited chicken. The woman was always doing strange things, but she wasn't doing them alone. The transparent image of another woman danced with her.

Other ghosts milled about the yard, like a

layer of the past overlaid onto the present, with only Polly interacting between the two. Two men in cowboy hats walked out of what used to be the barn. A woman hung laundry on an invisible clothesline that disappeared the second she let go of it. Another woman worked her arms up and down as if drawing water from an invisible well. A child ran from the house as she chased a boy. A man watched them from the kitchen window, smiling.

They were the moments from life that probably meant very little at the time, an ordinary day, an ordinary task, a locked instant.

Lily wanted to speak, but she couldn't find words. A chill crept up the back of her neck. It beckoned her to look, but she didn't want to see. Someone stood close to her back.

Polly's dance partner smiled, curtseyed, and then blurred into oblivion.

The feeling behind her didn't go away, and Lily finally made her body turn. Part of her knew before she even looked.

Marigold.

Lily was not prepared for the emotions that welled inside her, bursting out of that little seed she kept buried deep to take over everything else.

Marigold looked as she remembered her

from childhood, with auburn hair flowing down her back and kind hazel eyes—not the crazy lady drawing symbols on her window, not the junkie trying to score as her kids waited in the car. Knowing magic was real did not change that reality. Or did it? Could her mother have been under a magical spell, jonesing for a kind of infusion that Lily didn't understand?

No. That was wishful thinking. Lily knew what she knew. Unless magic was being peddled in every major city's back alley by some shady dude with greasy hair, and involved tiny plastic bags with powdery residue, her mother had been fighting a very human demon. If magic drove Marigold to that dark place, it didn't really matter. The facts remained. The woman fell down a rabbit hole of self-destruction, abandoned her children, and…

And a part of Lily would always love the woman despite all of it.

Reality wasn't only those bad memories Lily clung to. There was more to her legacy. More to Marigold Crawford Goode.

This woman had been her childhood—the youthful face, the smile, the laugh. How could she have forgotten the laugh? They had been a happy family once.

Marigold's arm moved and Lily looked down to see a hand caressing a pregnant belly. When she looked back up, Marigold's face had changed. Her hair was shorter and wrinkles fanned her eyes. She was no longer smiling. This broken, sad creature was how Lily remembered her mother.

"Mom?" Lily whispered, reaching out to touch her.

That one word seemed to break a spell. Marigold disappeared, taking the layer from the past with her. The ghosts faded. The talking around her became louder, as if it had been there all along, only she couldn't hear it.

"—all clear. You'll want to have that heat damage checked out as quickly as possible." The burly firefighter who spoke didn't wait for a confirmation.

"We seriously need to look at getting Polly a wellness check or something," Dante said. "I mean, eccentric is one thing. I think Polly might have passed that and gone straight into madness with that chicken dance over there."

"Polly's fine. She knows what she's doing," Lily dismissed.

"Hey, what's wrong with you? Normally you joke with me." Dante placed a hand on her shoulder. "Talk to me."

"I saw Mom."

"Marigold?"

"Mom," Lily repeated.

"We never call her that," Dante said.

"I saw her," Lily insisted.

"She's not dead?"

"Mom. I saw *Mom*." Lily tried to think of the words to explain what had happened, but the feelings were still too overwhelming for her. "She was standing right here. I saw her. And she was..."

"Marigold's ghost is here?" Dante looked around as if he could somehow detect the spirit. "I'm so sorry, Lily. That sucks. When will your bad luck be over?"

"Oh, sugar bee." Polly appeared, petting her arm.

"She's gone," Lily whispered.

"Is she haunting the place?" Dante asked. "Do you think she'll come back?"

"That's not the kind of gone she means, Florus," Polly said, her voice soothing. "Yes, sugar bee, she's gone."

A tear slid down Lily's cheek. It had been easier to hold on to anger, to not face this moment. When their mother had been alive, there was always that tiny hope, that chance that things could be repaired. Lily hadn't expected the wave of grief that washed over her. It seized hold of her stomach and tightened over her heart. For a second, she felt like she couldn't breathe.

"What did she tell you?" Polly asked.

Lily shook her head. The ghost hadn't spoken.

"Not with words. What did she tell you?" Polly insisted.

"She was young." Lily tried to inhale deeply but her lungs physically did not want to obey. "She must have been pregnant. Then she wasn't pregnant, and she looked like the last time I saw her."

"What does it mean?" Polly asked.

"Goodbye? Reminding me of how she was my mother? I don't know." How was Lily supposed to interpret the actions of her mother's ghost?

"Try not to think about it, Lily. Nothing good will come of it." Dante sloshed through the muddy backyard toward his phone. "This is a mess. I can't believe they just left it like this."

"We're Goodes. They don't want to help us." Exhaustion filled every inch of her as Lily examined the back of the house. There had been mishap after mishap since they'd come to this unlucky place. She was a fool to think she could ever have a business here. The first night, her guests could be lit on fire, or possessed, or tripped by gnomes. "Maybe the locals are right. Maybe we are the problem. We're the curse. We're the bad luck that's infecting the town."

"We didn't do this," Dante disagreed.

"Florus is right," Polly said.

"Look what has happened since we moved into this damned death trap. Lights falling, barns burning, threats, exploding milkshakes, hungry ghosts who want to eat Herman and date Aunt Polly, and—"

"Wait." Dante held up his hands to stop her tirade. "What exploding milkshakes? When did we have milkshakes?"

"Nothing good has come from us being here. So we're witches, so what? That has only brought with it more trouble. Even if we learn to control our magic, you can't tell me there won't be consequences to using it."

"Everything in life has consequences, sugar bee, even magic." Polly looped her arm through Lily's and pulled her toward the house. "Come inside. I'll make you spaghetti squash."

"No. We can't stay here, Polly. It's not safe. You should get Herman and we'll check back into the mice hotel."

"Oh, they caught the mice family," Polly said.

"I should have made us leave long before now." When it looked like they would protest, she said, "It's my house. No one stays."

"Jeez, way to pull rank," Dante mumbled. "I'll grab a bag."

Chapter Twenty

Who wants us gone?

Who wants us dead?

Where in the world did Nolan run off to and why?

For whatever reason that last question vexed Lily the most. He'd said something before he left, but she hadn't heard it in her foggy state. Still, she would have liked it if he had stayed. In the diner, there had been times when she'd thought he might actually kiss her again.

Out of all the mysteries she needed to solve, why Nolan Dawson didn't kiss her and hang around after her house nearly burned down shouldn't be at the top of her list.

Lily felt like she needed to do something, so she walked to the hotel room window and gazed out over the parking lot to the highway beyond. Polly and Herman shared a room next door. Oddly, the clerk who checked them in didn't blink twice at someone adding a pet lobster to the guest list. Dante's room was right above hers. She heard him walking above her every once in a while.

She balanced her cellphone on her shoulder as it rang. She waited for Alice MacIver to pick up. The attorney never failed to answer her biggest client.

"MacIver Law," Alice greeted.

"Hey, it's Lily. I just wanted to give you a heads up that we're not staying at the house anymore. The trust or whoever probably needs to be made aware."

The panicked catch of Alice's breath was so evident that Lily could practically feel the apprehension radiating through the phone. "Is this because of the citations?"

"Citations?" It took Lily a moment to remember what the lawyer was talking about. "Oh, you mean Marcel Proust's *Remembrance of Things Past.*"

"I'm sorry?" Alice clearly didn't get Lily's humor.

"World record holder for the longest book. The stack of citations is impossibly huge and painful to read, kind of like a Proust novel... you know what, never mind. It's not important." Jokes weren't funny if a person had to explain them.

"I want you to know I'm working on it. Please don't leave town yet." Poor Alice. She was so scared of losing the Goode trust as a client.

"Working on what?" Lily leaned her head against the glass and watched a married couple walk toward the front entrance of the hotel through the streetlights. At least, she assumed they were married. They looked the type—same style of his-and-hers clothing and matching designer luggage. The husband strode ahead while the wife had a very animated conversation with his back. To herself, she said, "Oh, that's sad. Fighting on vacation. They should make up."

"I am sure we have a case for the misuse of power. Lucky Valley officials have no right to try to run you out of town. I promise you. I am handling it. That is what you pay me for. I am on your side."

Lily dropped the curtain. She didn't like the sick feeling churning inside her. "What do you mean Lucky Valley officials want to run us out of town?"

"Apparently, when they expanded the city

limits to include the Goode property, they not only necessitated that the house be brought up to code, but if enough time passed without someone claiming the property, they would have been able to get a legal injunction that would give them the right to tear down the house and outbuildings and annex the property."

"The city wants to take my house?" Lily again peeked outside. Clouds rolled across the sky, blocking out the stars and moon, darkening the landscape even more. Only the tall lights over the parking lot allowed her to see. "They can't do that."

Maybe she should save everyone the trouble and just give it to them? No more death threats or headaches. If the whole town hated them so much, maybe it was time to leave.

"I'm conferring with a friend who's more versed in these kinds of property disputes. There are certain circumstances where Eminent Domain can be claimed by the government if it's deemed for the public good. Or they can force the sale of abandoned property, which is what I think they were trying to accomplish. To keep the house in your family, you need to live there." Alice sighed. "You can't leave. If you do, and the house is not brought up to code, you could lose everything. When the trust was set up, there wasn't a provision for this. With no property to oversee, all assets remaining in the Goode trust will be tied up in courts while it's all sorted out. Trust laws have changed since the late 1800s. I assure you, I'm livid. Lucky Valley officials had no right to instruct the city code enforcer to try to muscle you out of your rightful inheritance."

"Are you telling me that the town of Lucky Valley ordered the city code enforcer to run us out of town? First they gave us a giant list of nonsense and told us we have to fix it, and when that didn't scare us off, they vandalized the property and threatened us?" Lily nearly choked on the words. Could it really be that simple?

Had Nolan left with the deputy to regroup and plan? Is that why the deputy refused to help them? Herczeg was employed by the town. The lawn fire happened the first night Nolan came over. Had he been inside distracting them? And today? Was their trip to the diner a way to get her out of the house so someone could torch the place?

"I promise, I am working to get to the bottom of this." Alice tried to sound reassuring.

"Lucky Valley hired Nolan Dawson to get rid of me?" Lily needed to hear the woman say it was Nolan. She didn't want to believe it.

"I'm sorry. I hadn't heard there was

vandalism as well. Send me any police reports and receipts and I'll make sure it's taken care of. Anything you need, just—"

"Thank you for telling me, Alice," Lily interrupted. "I'll let you know what we decide."

Lily's hand shook as she flipped the phone closed to end the call, cutting the attorney off mid-farewell.

All along, it was Nolan.

Nolan.

Dammit. She had not seen that one coming.

Logically, it all fit, all the pieces. Why hadn't she seen it? How could she have been so stupid? All the construction accidents they were having, what better person than the guy who was supposed to fix things? He offered to help so he could... what? Keep a close eye on things? Sabotage any progress? Summon ghosts?

Break her heart?

Lily didn't want to believe it, but Alice had no reason to lie. It was in the attorney's best interest to have them stay. Nolan had tried to convince her to leave Lucky Valley several times.

A thud sounded behind the curtain and Lily jumped in fright. Something knocked a few times, and she edged closer to peek outside. She sighed in momentary relief. The married couple that had been fighting moments before now made out against the glass, kissing and fondling. Lily pounded several times to get their attention. The husband's eyes met hers briefly, and the wife giggled as he led her away.

Lily stared at a smudged handprint the husband had left behind on the glass. How could she have been so wrong about Nolan? She felt betrayed, disappointed, sad.

No. That wasn't right. She felt heartbroken.

Lily closed her eyes. She wanted to know why he had done it. She'd trusted him. He was going to be her business partner. He was her friend.

"Welcome to Lucky Valley, home of bad luck. Everything here really *is* cursed."

Chapter Twenty-One

Lily opened her eyes to look at the parking lot. She didn't know how long she'd stood, waiting for Alice to call to say she'd made a mistake. It wasn't Nolan who'd betrayed her. That call never came.

Lily stared at her hand pressed to the glass. Slowly, the feeling of the window against her hand turned to air, and the view of the parking lot became a small living room. It was not a place that she recognized. She lowered her hand.

Dammit. She'd teleported again.

A streetlight came in through a window, giving just enough light to make out shadowed details. The teal blue couch had a pleather finish and matched the overstuffed chair next to it. A print of some obscure impressionist painting hung over it. The chest that doubled as a coffee table had a basket with pinecones. Lily could detect no clues as to where she had transported herself, only that she was technically committing a crime by breaking into the home.

Thank goodness she was wearing clothes and shoes and hadn't been sleeping. She wasn't sure she could explain standing in her underwear in someone's house.

The house was quiet, and she prayed the homeowners were gone. Then she prayed she was still in Lucky Valley, or at least Colorado, or at the very least the United States. Wood floors were covered by large oval rugs, the woven kind Ronald and Ila Whaylen had all over their farmhouse. The thick brown strands coiled around from the center, wrapping around themselves like a snake. Lily used to walk the oblong patterns, around and around, placing her feet carefully as she pretended to balance on a tightrope.

When she shifted her weight, the boards beneath her creaked. She held her breath, listening to see if someone stirred. Her senses were honed, so focused that each breath felt like a scream.

Shadowed doorways led from the living

room. One appeared to lead toward a kitchen, another a hall. The wooden front door had a diamond window cut out of the top. It was close, but the creaking floor sounded like an alarm each time she moved.

Lightning flashed outside, momentarily illuminating the room. Five seconds later, thunder boomed. The storm would be about a mile away, and so far there was no sound of rain.

Lily took it slowly. A small table next to the door held several pieces of mail. She tried to read the labels in the dim light. Lifting a piece of junk mail toward the diamond window, she read, "Dawson, Nolan."

This was Nolan's house?

She dropped the envelope and turned back around. "Nolan?"

A thud answered her call.

"Nolan, it's Lily. I need to talk to you."

A second thud.

She followed the sound, no longer caring about the noise she made. She went into the kitchen. An artificial light came through a cracked door which led down to a basement.

"Nolan, I need some answers." Lily didn't hesitate to go down the wooden steps. His red flannel shirt was at the bottom of the stairs next to an undershirt. The musty smell of stones and earth greeted her. As she passed below the main level floor, the view opened up.

Deputy Herczeg lay on her back, her arms splayed. Her eyes were closed, and a large gash bled along her collarbone.

Lily didn't stop to think as she hurried to the woman's side. As she tried to kneel, a dark movement passed close to her face. She felt the air sweep against her skin.

A low growl punctured the silence.

Lily froze, terrified. She should have looked before leaping to the deputy's rescue. Following the sound with her eyes, she came face to face with a werewolf.

There was no mistaking what it was. The fur-covered body, the elongated snout and mouthful of fanged teeth. Hot breath panted against her skin. It swiped for her again and she screamed, falling back. One manacle held the wolf by a wrist as three more hung free. It looked like the deputy had tried to chain Nolan to the wall and failed.

"Full moon," Lily whispered. At the time, she hadn't been able to hear him as his lips moved. "That's what you said to me earlier. Full moon."

The werewolf strained against his chain.

"Nola—?"

The word was cut short by a loud growl which ended in a bark.

"Okay, okay." She tried to catch her breath. "You're not Nolan. Not right now."

The wolf panted. Yellow eyes focused on her. Animalistic rage radiated off him. The wolf was everything Nolan wasn't.

"Deputy Herczeg?" Lily whispered. She shook the woman's leg. The deputy didn't move.

Nolan growled and slapped his paw down close to the deputy's shoulder. The woman had fallen just out of his reach. He jerked against the chain as if he'd tear off his own arm to be free.

Lily grabbed the deputy by the leg and pulled her toward the stairs. Herczeg's arms flailed above her head. Blood trailed behind her on the floor.

Nolan howled.

Lily hoisted the deputy up and hooked her under each arm. Her muscles strained as she tried dragging the woman up the wooden stairs one at a time.

"Okay, we got this," Lily said, pausing to pull up another step. "One at a time."

The deputy gasped as her body slumped.

Lily lost her footing and slipped back. She fell on her backside, nearly losing the deputy down the stairs.

"Easy, I got you." Lily clung to the woman. "We need to get you out of here."

Herczeg looked around in confusion before calming enough to stop fighting Lily's help. "I didn't finish getting him in the trap. I have to go back and—"

"Oh, no, no, no," Lily denied. "I can't let you go back down there. One arm is chained. That will have to do."

"If he gets free…" The deputy flinched and reached for her wound.

"The only way we're going back down there is if you have a tranq dart big enough to put down an elephant." Lily didn't give the woman a choice as she hoisted her upward to stand on her feet.

"Tranq dart wouldn't work on him," the deputy answered.

They stumbled their way upstairs. Once in the kitchen, Lily slammed the basement door. Her tailbone felt broken as she limped to the sink on a twisted ankle. Rain had started and now pounded the window in front of the sink, obscuring the scene beyond. Lightning flashed, followed by thunder. She searched the drawers and found a clean dishtowel. Wetting it, she went back to where the deputy leaned against the wall. She pressed the damp towel to the wound.

"Hey," Deputy Herczeg protested, even as she grabbed the towel to hold it in place. She took several breaths through the pain. "You don't understand. That one chain might not be enough to hold him. It's a full moon."

"It will have to be." Lily looked at her hands. "Or, I guess I'll have to figure out how this magic thing works."

The deputy chuckled though the laugh held no humor. "You don't know anything, do you?"

"What?"

"He's a Dawson werewolf."

"You're right, I apparently don't know what that means." Lily grabbed another dishtowel and looped it under the deputy's arm to tie the other towel into place. "Not perfect, but we need to keep pressure on that wound until we can get you to the hospital. Where's a phone? We need to call an ambulance."

"I can't go to the hospital."

"You have to. That cut is deep."

"I can't leave." The deputy grunted in pain. "Dawson wolves are one of the feral bloodlines. They're not like other wolves. All month long they're great people, sometimes too great, and when they shift into wolves, for the most part they're still fine. Except for once a lunar month on the full moon, when all that pent-up anger or frustration, or whatever it is normal people carry around inside of them, just rushes out. The animal emerges, and the man disappears. They call it the Dawson curse. There's a whole section about it in the law enforcement handbook. If you can't get a Dawson wolf into a trap by the rise of the full moon, the only other option is to shoot to kill."

"But I'm a Goode. You said it yourself. Maybe I can——"

"Some say it was the Goodes who cursed the bloodline, but all say there is nothing that can stop it. Every attempt to end the curse has failed. Nolan's own father broke his chains and had to be put down while he terrorized a bus full of teenagers." The deputy held her arm. "I can't leave. I have to make sure he's contained."

"I'm not letting you hurt him." Lily limped to stand between the basement and the deputy.

"If he doesn't get free, I won't."

"I'll stay. You need to get to the hospital." Needlessly, Lily pulled the door handle to ensure the latch was engaged and it was closed.

"You go. I have a job to——"

The deputy's words cut off abruptly and Lily spun around, thinking the woman had passed out from the pain. Herczeg was gone.

"Deputy?"

The shout only caused Nolan to howl.

Lily hurried to look in the living room. The deputy wasn't there. Had she magically expelled the deputy from the house?

"Think, Lily. Protect yourself." She automatically reached to find her phone, but it was back at the hotel. She thought about what Herczeg said regarding Nolan's father. In his current condition, Nolan was not Nolan. He was dangerous. She had seen it for herself, the wolf's uncontrollable rage. Lily opened the kitchen drawers, searching for a weapon. Taking out a butcher's knife, she hopped to the table and sat down, facing the basement door. Her tailbone and ankle throbbed, but she didn't dare take her eyes away from the door.

Seeing the blade in her shaking hands, she set it down and slid it away. There was no way she could ever use it on a living creature. She lifted her ankle and gingerly placed it on her knee. It was starting to turn purple and swell.

She pointed her fingers at it. "Heal."

It still throbbed.

"I command you to stop hurting." She flicked her hands at the appendage. Then, desperate, she tried to talk like Polly. "Boodgy boo, squishy too, heal."

Not surprising, speaking nonsense didn't work either.

She grabbed her calf and leaned her head against the tabletop. Grumbling, she said, "This day sucks. Is it too much to ask that my backside and ankle heal themselves?"

Heat infused her injuries, burning so hot she yelped in surprise and sat up straight in the chair. The pain lessened until it went away completely. She checked her foot, rolling the ankle. The swelling was gone. She wiggled in her chair. Her bottom was fixed as well.

"Thank you." She sighed in relief. Now with that taken care of, she could try to come up with a plan that didn't involve knives.

Eyeing the width of the floor space between the basement door to the wall, she stood and began looking around the home. The teal couch was about the right length. Lily shoved Nolan's furniture aside and tossed the woven rug out of her way. She forcefully slid the couch across the wood floor through the path she'd created. Her feet slipped under the weight, but she kept pushing. The kitchen doorway was a tight fit, and the material ripped along the back seam.

Once she made it to the kitchen, it was easier. She forced one arm of the couch against the basement door and then wedged the opposite arm against the wall to create a blockade. The length of the couch jammed the door closed.

Breathing hard, she studied her handiwork. She had no idea if that would be enough to stop a werewolf, but it should at least slow him down. She heard thumping coming from the basement, followed by low growls and scratches. Chain links rattled.

Lily crawled over the back of the couch so she could sit against the arm while facing the door. It was more comfortable than the kitchen chair. Now all she had to do was wait the curse out.

IT WASN'T the noise that pulled Lily from the haze of sleep, but silence. She'd dozed off to the sounds in the basement. It had been comforting to know that the wolf was chained. Now, in the silence, all she heard was her body brushing against the couch and the sound of her breath.

Was it over?

A quick glance toward the window over the sink revealed the sky was dark, but not black. Had early morning ended the curse?

Lily crawled forward and leaned toward the

door. She turned her head, listening as she inched closer slowly.

Crash!

Wood splintered, flying toward her face. Her uplifted hand blocked some of the shards, protecting her. She pushed back, slamming herself into the wall in fright.

A clawed hand reached for her, swinging violently through the hole. The couch quaked as the werewolf shoved his weight into the door.

"Nolan, stop!" Lily felt her hands tingle, but nothing happened. What was the point of magic if it never worked when you needed it to?

Claws ripped the couch as if he tried to anchor himself so he could pull through the broken door. The wood creaked, and she knew it wouldn't hold much longer.

Lily scrambled to get out of the way and fell to the floor by the back of the couch. She crawled toward the table in search of the knife. "I don't want to hurt you. Nolan, can you hear me? Please don't make me hurt you."

The sound of her voice only seemed to make the creature angrier. She wanted to run. She needed to stay. Deputy Herczeg had been clear. If he escaped, he'd hurt everyone he came across. She stayed on the floor and reached over her head to feel the tabletop. Her hand bumped the knife handle, and she scrambled to pick up the weapon.

Everything since that first phone call from Aunt Polly had become upside-down. This was not how things were supposed to go. Nothing in Lucky Valley was what she'd expected. The town was right. This place was cursed with bad luck. Now her bad luck was going to force her to stop Nolan or die trying. One of them would not be leaving here.

Nolan shoved his head through a hole in the cracked wood. His angry eyes met hers and he snarled violently. His body thrashed to be free.

"Please stop," she whispered. She dug her heels into the floor, pressing tight against the wall as she used the table to hide from his view even as she leaned to the side to watch. It took all her willpower to keep her eyes open. "I can't let you leave. I can't let you leave."

The door broke apart and Nolan surged through with a howl. The momentum sent his weight flying forward. He slammed into the wall and then landed where she couldn't see him in front of the couch. Lily clutched the knife. She held her breath and waited. Her hands shook as she held the weapon like a sword before her.

Any second. She had to be ready.

Any second.

Any...

"Nolan?" she whispered.

Nothing.

"Nolan, please, don't..." Lily grabbed hold of the table and used it to steady herself as she stood. She crept toward the couch, stepping gingerly on the pieces of the door.

Nolan lay unmoving, wedged into the narrow space between the front of the couch and the wall, half-shifted. The bulging muscles had smoothed, taking the fur with it. Claws slowly retracted into his fingers.

It was over. As the werewolf faded, it left a naked man in its place.

She looked out the window. There was enough light to indicate dawn.

Lily threw the knife away from her. It skidded under the table. She crawled over the couch and touched his hand. This time her voice was firm. "Nolan." He gave a light moan. "Nolan, wake up."

His head lifted and his eyes lazily opened to meet hers. "Lily? What...?" He pushed against the couch cushion to free himself from the tight fit. "What are you doing here? What happened?" His eyes took in the disheveled kitchen, then the fact he was naked. He instantly cupped his hands in front of his privates. A broken chain hung from one wrist. "What did I do?"

Lily glared at him. "You know what you did."

"Did I hurt you?" He started to reach for her, only to think better of it as he kept his hand shield where it was. "Why are you here?"

The intimacy of the early morning light and his naked skin wasn't helping her concentration. She climbed back over the couch to put distance between them. "I came to tell you that you're fired. I know you were hired by the town council to sabotage the house. I know that you're partly to blame for all the accidents that have been happening. I know why that Councilman Rana was so desperate to get you on the phone."

"Who told you that?" Nolan shook his head, denying her accusations. She turned to leave. "Lily, don't go. I can explain."

"What's to explain? I'm a Goode. Every step of the way, I've been told what that means in this town. I thought you were different. I thought you were my friend, but you're not. I should have realized something was up the moment you handed me that stack of citations. You've wanted us gone from the beginning. The townsfolk... I can understand their fear of us. They don't know us. They only know stories of my crazy ancestors. But you, Nolan? You know better. You know me.

I've never lied to you. I've never hidden who I was or what I wanted."

"Wait, Lily."

This time he did reach for her, but she strode out of the kitchen, only to call back, "I'm sorry I trashed your house trying to keep you locked in the basement. I guess that makes us a little even."

Chapter Twenty-Two

Nolan strode down Main Street. His truck was in the shop, so he had no other way to get around. It didn't matter. He'd walk all the way to Lily's house if he had to. He knew she was mad and couldn't blame her. The city had asked him to chase her off, and he had initially agreed. But after the citations, he'd stopped.

Lily didn't deserve the trouble that came her way. She deserved a chance to open her bed and breakfast, or whatever else she wanted to do with the family property. She was nothing like her ancestors were rumored to be.

Hearing a vehicle rolling up behind him, he kept walking. Deputy Herczeg pulled alongside him and kept pace. "Glad to see you in one piece."

"Thanks for the ride last night."

"Get in. I'll give you a lift." She stopped the vehicle.

He walked a few steps before stopping and coming back around. "I'm going to the Goode Estate."

"I figured. So am I." The deputy motioned at him to get in.

As they drove down Main Street, he asked, "Did you tell Lily the council wanted me to run her out of town?"

"Why would I? I have no reason to." Herczeg glanced at him. "The council ordered me not to help her. They promised me that you wouldn't hurt her, only scare her. I need this job, and I believe I best serve the public by getting the Goode family out of town. Things have become weird since they've arrived. Last night, we had a full-on epidemic of lunar sickness. The emergency room was over capacity. The O'Donnell twins tried to put on a naked Shakespearean play by the mermaid statue. Cherry had a psychic episode and stalled fifteen cars on the interstate —all tourists, of course, one couple who was convinced it was because of aliens."

Nolan nodded toward her shoulder. "Is that why you have a bandage?"

"No. Some idiot forgot it was the full moon

and didn't get into his trap in time." She gave him a side-eyed look.

He winced. "The good news is, my werewolf gene isn't contagious. It should heal normally."

"I already checked," Herczeg assured him. She lifted her left hand to show a bandage on her wrist. "I'm actually more concerned by the Echidna bite."

"Echidna came out of her cave?" Nolan shivered. The snake lady was rarely seen, and everyone preferred it that way.

"She was cranky as hell, too." The deputy drove out of town. "That ogre nurse, Ulga, said a scaly rash is a common side effect, and she doesn't know how to stop it. The skin is already turning green. She said my only course of action was to find a powerful witch and hope they knew what to do. As much as I hate to do it, I'm heading out to the Goode Estate to see if they have anything that can help. I don't have much of a choice at this point."

"If they can, they will," Nolan assured her, though he would understand if the Goode family didn't want to. It's not like the deputy had been too willing to help the witches in the past. "The town council is wrong. Lily Goode and her family aren't here to hurt us. She wants to make a life here, start a business, set down roots."

"I don't think she's a bad person, but I do know the bad luck returned with her." Herczeg slowed as a car came barreling toward them. She eyed the driver as they passed and jerked her thumb several times in a downward motion to signal at him to slow down. The driver slammed on his brakes and skidded to a more reasonable speed. "I think she's safer with you trying to get her out, otherwise someone else might decide to take matters into their own hands."

"You think I'm responsible for the graffiti and fires?" Nolan shook his head. "The only thing I did was write up a stack of legal citations."

"So, if it wasn't you, who? Did the council send someone else?" Herczeg increased their speed. "They only told me you were involved. They wanted to keep it quiet."

"I don't know. I thought so until the fire yesterday. That wasn't a scare tactic. That was someone trying to do actual damage. The pour patterns on the ground were unmistakable. They wanted the barn fire to light the house. There's nothing clean about an insurance investigation, and the city can't consider a house that's no longer standing as abandoned. The law is different when it comes to land. Tracts fall under wildlife preservation and there would be nothing the town could do to seize the property. This was not someone working for the council."

"If it wasn't you, then that means there's a real threat after them." The deputy drove faster. "I may not want the Goode family in town, but I don't want to see them harmed on their way out, either."

Nolan gripped his hand into a tight first. It now made sense why Herczeg wasn't too helpful when it came to her investigations. It should have occurred to him to talk frankly with her before now. He willed the woman to drive faster.

Chapter Twenty-Three

"Stop trying so hard to control everything," Polly scolded.

Lily wasn't sure if her aunt was talking to her, the lobster, or the three gnomes standing on the dining room table. She had her back to the woman while she stared at the ruined kitchen. The smell of smoke and char lingered in the air. The fire had breached the exterior wall alongside the window frame, creating a hole Lily could see daylight through. It had burnt its way onto the cabinets, streaking them with soot all the way to the ceiling. Water from the firehose had saturated the area. It pooled into the dining room and living room, watermarking the floor.

How could Nolan have done this to them? She'd trusted him.

"Are you listening to me, sugar bee?" Polly asked.

"No." It wasn't a lie. She hadn't been paying attention. Footsteps sounded upstairs, and she assumed it was her brother checking for damage on the second floor.

"The reason why your magic keeps misfiring is because you're trying too hard to control it. It's like breathing. When you're not thinking about breathing, it happens as it's meant to. When you concentrate on it, the act stops being automatic, you lose your rhythm, and you need the practice to find it again. Magic and mind must become one."

"Whatever you say, sensei," Lily answered. Thank goodness the trust was paying for the damage. Maybe now that she knew about the council trying to run her out of town, all this nonsense would stop.

Feeling a chill, she looked at the back door. Stan stood with a big grin on his face as he stared at Polly. He took off his hat and smoothed down his hair like he was about to ask her on a date. A glance at her aunt told Lily the woman didn't appear to see the ghost. When she looked back, Stan met her eyes. He slapped his hat on his leg and cackled before he disappeared.

"…new luck potion is about ready," Polly was

saying. Lily had stopped paying attention again and had to force herself to listen. "We'll be able to help with the worst cases of bad luck in town if we can get them to agree to take it."

"That could go a long way toward creating goodwill within the…" Lily's words trailed off as she caught movement in the window. The image of her pregnant mother stood on the lawn, facing the barn, just as she had the first time Lily saw her. "Mom."

"Marigold is here?" Polly rushed to her side. "Herman, be a good boy—and darn it, Lugwick get out of his water. Herman can't play right now. You two behave. I'll be right back."

Lily hurried out the back door. The ground was still damp from the evening before. She ran through the mud. "Mom?"

Marigold stared at the collapsed barn. The ghost didn't acknowledge her.

"Marigold." Lily tried to get her attention. The pregnant belly faded away as did her mother's youth. Lily stopped in front of the ghost. Perhaps Marigold's manifestation hadn't been a message for Lily to remember the good with the bad. Maybe her mother was simply locked in some kind of spiritual purgatory. Polly joined her on the yard. "Polly, do you see her?"

"No. I can feel her, but her message isn't for

me." Polly lifted her hands as if detecting the general area where Marigold stood. "Hello, old friend."

If Marigold heard, she didn't let on.

"Tell me what you see," Polly said.

"Same as last time. She's pregnant and young, and then she's not." Lily looked around. "She's fixated on where the barn used to stand."

"Oh, clever, clever woman," Polly said.

"Do you understand her?" Lily couldn't take her eyes off her mother's face, even as the woman seemed to gaze through her.

"No, but whatever it is, it's very clever," Polly answered.

"Maybe it's the barn?" Lily had a hard time walking away from the ghost, but she went toward the rubble. To her, it was simply a charred, wet, broken pile of junk. "Did my mom have a thing for barns?"

"Not that I can remember. She did enjoy almonds though," Polly answered.

A chill worked over Lily. It was a sensation she was beginning to recognize. More ghosts were coming.

She turned to see that the white humanoid blurs were back. Their expressions began to take shape, filling in until she could see their faces. Most of them were men in dirty overalls and large jackets. Their brimmed hats came in a variety of shapes. The feral black cat appeared close by, hissing at the ghosts.

A man at the front of the gathering had a gaping wound in his head, which he covered with a hat. His thick mustache stretched down his cheeks. Anger brewed in his eyes. This was not like the blurry figures of before. Their bodies were dense, losing their transparency.

This was definitely not something she could blame on Nolan.

They were the miners from the accident long ago. Nolan had said a hundred and eighteen workers had died in the collapse. As she scanned over the spirit gathering, she silently started estimating their numbers.

Six. Ten. Twenty. Fifty. Too many…

"Polly," Lily whispered. "I think we need to run."

"Naked in the moonlight? Yay!" Polly clapped her hands. Ethereal eyes turned toward her aunt at the sound. "Exercise is—"

"No, Polly, ghosts. Angry ghosts." She kept her voice low. "Like a hundred of them."

Something clanked in the distance, metal chipping away at rock, one strong strike and then a skitter like a metal tip bouncing.

Lily grabbed Polly's wrist and pulled. The

woman shivered violently, slipping free. Angry mustache ghost moved, the step more like a glide. Lily reached for Polly a second time. They needed to run.

"Oh, dear, I see what you mean," Polly said, as if Lily's touch had cleared her vision to what was happening around them. "What do they— oh, hello, Marigold. There you are."

The clank sounded again. Each miner took a step forward and then stopped, commanded by the sound.

"Who's doing that?" Polly scolded. "Everyone knows that ghost armies are forbidden in accordance with the Compostella Treaty of 1457."

"What are you talking about? Nobody knows that." Lily forced the woman to back away with her.

"What, then, are they teaching you kids in school?" Polly clicked her tongue in disappointment.

The clank of metal on stone struck again, repeating several times.

"What do we do?" Lily asked her aunt. She looked up at the house, trying to detect her brother in the windows. He wasn't there, and she didn't want to call out to him and let the ghosts know he was nearby.

"Get behind the gnomes," her aunt ordered.

"Aunt Polly, I'm being serious."

"Sugar bee, so am I. I told you it never hurts to have an army of garden gnomes protecting your property, especially a house as magical as this one." She motioned toward the side yard.

The small statues were lined up in rows where before there had been empty grass and mud. They were all there—toilet gnome reading his paper, gnomes holding baskets and flowers, cross-legged gnome, one hiding under a ceramic mushroom, the mother and her gnome baby... all of them. The gnome from the front porch held a sign in front of the formation that read, "*To the ready*." The black cat hid behind the back row.

"Gnomes versus ghosts?" Lily muttered in disbelief. "Today will not end well."

"Isn't it fascinating?" This time, Polly grabbed Lily's arm and pulled her from between the two armies. The clank sounded, and the ghosts advanced. The gnomes didn't move. Another clank. A miner wearing overalls with one strap undone stepped through her mother, causing Marigold to disappear.

And the gnomes did nothing.

Lily ran to the statues and grabbed toilet gnome. She held him over her head, ready to launch. Polly made a sharp noise of dismay and ran after her, jumping to pry the gnome from Lily's hands. She put him back in his place.

Polly lifted her arms and yelled, "Show yourself."

The clank stopped as did the ghosts the sound led to battle.

A figure moved through the ghost army. Lily leaned to the side. Long dark hair blew into her view. A woman dragged an old pickaxe on the ground.

It was the drifter from Unlucky Valley.

"Mara?" Lily asked in confusion. "I don't understand. What are you doing here?"

The woman didn't answer as she lifted the pickaxe over her head. She charged with a growl forming in her throat. As she brought the pickaxe down, the weapon veered to the left and struck the ground. The ghost army advanced.

"Is this about the other day? My brother is fine." Lily dodged as Mara swung again. "No one wants to hurt you. I promise."

"I don't want to hurt *you*," Mara said, "but I need you to leave this place."

"What you saw was a family misunderstanding," Lily tried to keep her tone reasonable. "It doesn't concern you."

"Of course it concerns me," Mara cried. Her eyes flashed with purple and gray, swirling as if possessed by a storm. "This is our land. We bled for it. We paid for it with bone!"

Was Mara one of them? Was she dead? They had found her in Unlucky Valley.

"What are you—?"

"And we will take it back!" Mara swung and missed several times, but that didn't stop her from trying until her arms could no longer lift the weapon.

"Polly, if your gnomes are going to do anything, now would be a great time," Lily insisted. Pregnant Marigold reappeared, just as unhelpful as before. Trust her mother to stand aside doing nothing as her children struggled to survive.

"I knew I had a bad feeling about her," Polly answered. "Mara is as sour as a bad pickle. You should have never brought her here, Lily."

Mara breathed hard, her gaze going from rigid to pleading. "It's getting difficult to hold the others back. It doesn't need to end like this. You can run. Just go. Don't come back to Lucky Valley. I tried to scare you away. I know you were trying to be kind when you invited me here and I left before they could make me... *argh*."

Mara's arms shook as she again lifted the pickaxe.

"You need to leave. Just leave. Let us have it,"

Mara cried, cracking her pickaxe down into the earth so hard, it lodged in place. "Too late."

The ghosts marched toward Lily, soundlessly attacking.

"Run!" Lily yelled.

Polly moved to stand in formation with the gnomes, squatting and holding very still in a strange pose.

Lily felt a cold hand grip her shoulder and another clamp around her ankle. The mob of spirits pulled her to the ground. Freezing cold invaded her body and stole her breath. Her lungs burned in need as the pressing mass of spectral bodies tried to suffocate her. She felt their anger, but also their fear. They were locked in a terrifying moment of the past. When they touched her, she was overcome with flashes of rocks falling and men screaming until the dust choked them. Her head became faint and she could no longer thrash as the energy drained out of her limbs.

Warmth found her arm in the cold cocoon. The touch gave her the energy she needed to ward off the spirits. Power pulsed out of her, expelling the ghosts from around her.

Mara screamed. Lily was pulled across the ground. She inhaled deeply, gasping for breath. She flung, fighting the hand that held her. She freed herself and began to crawl through the mud to safety.

"Lily, it's me, Nolan." Nolan was suddenly kneeling in front of her, holding her face in his hands. For a moment, she forgot what he'd done and was elated to see him. "Look at me. Breathe."

"They're coming," Lily managed to say. She tried to push past him. The feeling of death and fear still clung to her.

"Everyone, stop," Polly ordered. "I understand now. Marigold gave birth in the barn. That's what she was trying to say."

That didn't appear to be the message the ghosts wanted to get across. Lily highly doubted anyone cared where Marigold gave birth.

Lily looked back to see Polly rocking back and forth to pull the pickaxe from the ground. The second it released, and Polly held it in her hands, the ghost army dissipated. Her aunt tossed the weapon on the pile of barn rubble.

Mara lay on the ground, pushing up in a daze, only to fall down again. Whatever energy pulsed out of Lily had obviously incapacitated the woman. Her body seized, white mist coming out of her chest in the form of an angry miner. The spirit glared at her them before he too dispersed into thin air.

"That's better," Polly said with an audible sigh. "*Whew.*"

"I was born in a barn? How does that matter?" Lily frowned. She clung to Nolan when he tried to stand. He helped her to her feet and stayed close.

"You've been a bad girl, pickle." Polly stared down at Mara. She crossed her arms over her chest and shook her head like a disappointed school teacher.

"This house is ours," Mara mumbled defiantly, as if dazed. "I won't let it go. I don't care if the law says I'm not of Goode blood. I belong here."

"Lily, it's not safe here. Let me take your family into town and we can sort this out." Nolan tried to urge her away from the yard.

Lily ignored him and refused to follow. She shivered, still cold from where the ghosts had touched her. Her clothes were caked with mud and the weight pulled uncomfortably at her. "Will someone tell me what is going on? No more lies and secrets." She gave a pointed look at Polly. "And no more nonsensical explanations."

"All you need to know is that you're leaving, Lily Goode. They'll never let you keep this place." Mara sat up, but her arms hung slack by her sides, and she didn't pose much of a threat.

"We won't stop. We never stop. The dead don't sleep."

"Who is we?" Lily looked around. Nolan tried to hold on and his arms tightened around her shoulders. The ghost army had left. The useless gnomes were still in formation, doing nothing. Marigold's image was fading fast. "You're all alone."

"My family." Mara tilted her jaw downward but kept her gaze fixed on Lily. "My friends."

"Ghosts are not friends," Polly admonished. "I think you know this."

"I'll live here with my father," Mara insisted.

"No, pickle," Polly denied. "That will never happen. Your father is—"

"Will someone explain to me what is happening?" Lily practically shouted to be heard. She turned to Polly and demanded, "Who is this woman? What is she?"

"Lily, I'd like you to meet your half-sister, Amaryllis Clementine Goode." Polly relaxed her stance. "Isn't that right, Amaryllis?"

"Her name is Mara Edison from Albuquerque, New Mexico. She said she glowed in the dark as her supernatural power." Lily shook her head in denial, unable to believe what she was hearing. "It's obvious she's somehow connected to the ghost miners... maybe she's one of them?" She frowned at Mara. "Are you dead?"

"I'm only half dead on my father's side," Mara argued. Her voice became louder, and she shifted her weight on the ground. Her strength was returning.

"The lawyer said my youngest sister is dead," Lily continued, walking to stand over the woman, "and you even said you're not a Goode."

"No, I said my blood wasn't Goode blood. Joseph Goode wasn't my father, but Marigold was as much my mother as she was yours. She became pregnant after your father had his accident off the side of the quarry," Mara said. "That little fact does make it difficult to claim my childhood home. The family trust is all about being of the right blood, and the fact that mine is Crawford witch and not Goode, well…"

"This isn't funny." Nolan tried to stand protectively in front of Lily as if to shield her from the truth.

Lily didn't want his protection. Before she could answer, Deputy Herczeg came from the front of the house.

"Dante passed out on the porch but he's coming too," the deputy said. "There doesn't appear to be any injuries, but I put him in my vehicle." She came to a halt, instantly raising her hand and slowing her approach. She looked at the gnome formation and gave it a wide berth as she walked around it. "Would someone care to explain what's going on?"

No one answered the deputy's question.

"Arrest her. She's the one who's been vandalizing the house." Nolan pointed at Mara. "Trespassing, assault—"

Lily jerked away from him. "You're one to talk after what you did. Stay out of it."

"Lily," Nolan's tone pleaded with her to listen.

"Why are you even here, Nolan? I fired you. We don't need your input," Lily dismissed.

"I came here to explain," he said.

Lily ignored him and went cautiously toward her sister.

Mara pushed to her feet but appeared unsteady. Lily searched the woman's features, but Mara did not look like their mother. Their eyes met, and Mara glanced away first. Whatever had happened—or was happening to the woman— there was a much deeper story involved. She could not take things at face value. She needed answers. She was tired of the mystery surrounding everything in Lucky Valley.

Marigold reappeared. Mara limped over to the ghost and patted the pregnant belly, apparently able to touch the transparent figure. The stomach swirled like smoke, stirred by Mara's hand. "Polly is right. I was born in that barn. I was raised in this place." The stomach disappeared, and Marigold's face changed. "They say I did that to her. Having an evil spawn growing inside of her drove her to insanity."

"I've lived here my whole life," Nolan denied. "I've never seen you. I've never heard of you. If Marigold had a baby, people would have talked."

"Why do you think I was born in a barn? I always hated that place. I'm glad it's gone." Mara chuckled, though the sound held little humor. She winced and held her side. "I'm Marigold's little, dirty secret that she didn't want getting out."

Lily tried to feel a connection to the woman, but it was hard, especially when Mara had been swinging a pickaxe only moments before. "I'm sorry if our mother did something to you. She had issues. Some women aren't meant to be mothers, I guess. She abandoned me at a fire station with Jesse and Dante."

Mara pouted out her bottom lip and taunted, "Oh, poor Lily. Her mommy left her at a fire station to be raised by strangers. Boo-hoo. At least you had each other."

"Don't mock my pain," Lily warned. She felt her skin tingling as if magic tried to erupt.

"Our mother feared what my father's power had done to me, so she kept me locked away from other children. Sometimes in that barn like an animal. Sometimes, if I was good, she let me into the house. She was so scared I would harm other children if I was allowed out into the world. She said I suck the life out of everything I touch. It's true, too. You saw her. I sucked the life out of her. I can't be around people. I need this house—it's my home. The ghosts are my friends, my family. I can't leave them, and they are tied to this land."

Polly tried to say something, but Lily ignored her aunt.

"I am so sorry," Lily whispered. "I had no idea. I only learned I had another sister after I found out I was inheriting the estate."

"Am I the only one concerned by the fact that this woman just tried to kill Lily?" Nolan demanded. "We should—"

Lily frowned at him, cutting off his words.

"Mom couldn't lock me away from the ghosts. They could always find me." Mara rocked back and forth on her feet.

"You have to close the door, pickle," Polly stated.

"I could never beat them at hide-and-seek," Mara continued. "Especially when they hid inside me. At first, I would sleep, and they would play. Then I didn't need to sleep to let them in, thanks to my father."

"Who is your father?" Lily inched closer. Maybe the shape of Mara's eyes was like Marigold's. No, it wasn't that. They held the same wildness.

"A specter from Old Lucky Valley possessed a traveler and seduced our mother with spells and magic, and from that ill-fated union, I was born. The dead aren't supposed to have children with the living, and I'm the supernatural byproduct."

"Whatever our mother told you, it's wrong," Lily said. "And whatever happened to her was not your doing. Our mother was sick."

"No, Mara's right," Polly inserted. "The dead are not supposed to have children with the living. It's like tigers having babies with penguins."

"Polly," Lily scolded. She was doing her best not to antagonize Mara and keep the woman calm.

"Gee, thanks, I'm a *tiguin*," Mara drawled, "or a *penger*."

"Penger's cute," Polly said. "I like you much better like this, penger pickle, without all that extra baggage floating inside you. Your intentions are much easier to read now."

"Give me one reason why I shouldn't press charges? Make me understand, Mara," Lily said.

"Do what you have to." Mara crossed her arms over her chest.

"Oh, stop acting all tough." Polly waved a hand in dismissal. She turned her attention to Lily. "The vessel is empty. As long as it stays that way, she's harmless. Angsty and as annoying as a teenager, but harmless."

"I'm twenty," Mara said.

"You act like you're fifteen," Polly scolded. "I should have a potion to seal that door."

"We will take it back," Lily said.

"What?" Mara frowned at her.

"That's what you said. 'This is our land. We bled for it. We paid for it with bone. We will take it back.'" Lily finally began to put the pieces together. "You spoke for them, the ghosts. They bled. They died in those mines, not you. You're very much alive. It's like Polly said. You're some kind of vessel they use to... what? Feel human? Walk around in?"

Mara looked at the ground. "It's my purpose."

"No." Lily shook her head. "It's your burden. There was something about you I recognized the second we met, even though Nolan and Polly didn't trust you. I thought it was because I felt sorry for you since you reminded me of when I was your age—hungry and defensive. But now they no longer hide inside of you, I see that it's more than that. You're... broken."

Mara opened her mouth in defiance, but nothing came out. Instead, she licked her lips and stared at the barn.

"Marigold broke you, too." Lily took a deep breath. "It's like an invisible marker drawn all over your face."

"What's going on, and why was I in the back-seat of a police car? Did I do something to get arrested? Was I streaking through a football game again?" Dante held his head as he leaned against the corner of the scorched house. His eyes were a little glassy. "Wait, no, the last thing I remember was a knock and a creepy woman at the door. She made me all tingly when she touched me." He took a wobbly step forward and bumped a gnome. "Whoa, where did all of these come from? I swear they're multiplying."

Polly went toward Dante and sniffed him. She touched his chest and drew her hand quickly away. She shook her head in disapproval. "You opened the door to that knocker. She put all of her gracious hostess mojo on... *oh, tingly*." Polly wobbled on her feet and looked at her hand. She balled it into a fist and released it, not finishing her statement. A small smile came over her features. "It tickles."

"Man, seriously, you never open the door to a knocker," Mara said. "I can see she oozed her gunk all over your aura."

"Who are you?" Dante closed his eyes briefly and seemed to be struggling to remain upright.

"Our half-sister," Lily said.

"Another one?" Dante frowned, squinting at everyone in turn. "How many kids did Marigold have?"

"No, same one, only not completely dead," Lily answered.

"Amaryllis?" Dante asked in surprise. He pushed away from the house and strode to where Mara stood. Before she could defend herself, he hugged her. "I'm so happy to meet you. We only just learned about you and thought you were dead."

"What are you doing?" Mara struggled weakly, but he didn't let her go. Lily had the same question. What was her brother doing? Dante didn't hug strangers. Dante barely hugged her.

"You're a welcome addition to our—" Dante began.

"Seriously, why are you touching me?"

Mara dropped her shoulders and knees, trying to become dead weight, but it didn't work. "Sally's ectoplasm doesn't work on me. Get off, freak."

"Please tell me we have a brother, too," Dante begged. "I'm already the Y chromosome swimming in a sea of X's."

"Group hug!" Polly went and wrapped her arms around the two. "Lily, get over here."

Lily stayed beside Nolan. "Okay, Polly's always a little off. But, what the hell is wrong with Dante?"

"Sally appears to be highly contagious and spread by touch," Nolan said. "You should stay away from them."

The deputy scratched her head. "So, am I arresting anyone?"

"No," Polly said.

Deputy Herczeg looked at Lily expectantly.

"I guess not," Lily muttered.

"Is that a question?" The deputy held her bandaged wrist, the fist around it straining as it applied pressure.

"Yes, arrest these two." Mara groaned. "Get them off me."

"Lily, we have another sister," Dante exclaimed. "Isn't that wonderful?"

"Yes. Arrest Dante and put him in the drunk

tank or something until whatever this is goes away," Lily said. "Dante, get off—"

"No." Nolan held up his hand to stop Lily from going to her brother. "He let the knocker in. He's contagious. Don't touch him."

At the sound of Nolan's voice, Dante let go of Mara. Polly tried to hold on, but the girl flailed until she was free. It was clear by her expression, Mara was not used to being touched. Dante went to Nolan. He went to shake Nolan's hand, but Nolan drew away from his reach. "You'll make a fine brother. What do you say? Marry my sister and help me out with this handful of women?"

Lily gasped as her brother tried to marry her off.

"Well, I, ah—" Nolan stuttered.

"Oh my god, Dante, you are never allowed to answer the door again," Lily interrupted.

"Oh, a wedding, beautiful idea, Florus!" Polly clapped her hands. "The stars all say that next Tuesday is a perfect day for the joining of—"

"Stop," Lily cried, throwing her hands in the air. There were too many things happening, and she needed them all to be quiet and slow down so she could think. "All of you. Just stop it. I'm not getting married next Tuesday."

"I guess Thursday might work," Polly said.

Dante nodded to indicate he thought it was a good idea.

Lily paced away from Nolan and the others, putting distance between them. "No one is getting married on Thursday."

"Well, that's probably not technically true," Dante said.

"Florus has a point," Polly added.

"Are they always like this?" Mara also took a step back. "Because this seems extreme, even for a knocker, unless he was smeared with a massive dose."

"Polly yes, Dante no." Lily pushed wayward strands of hair out of her face.

"Lily, we need to go. We can't trust this woman." Nolan waved his hand toward Mara. "After everything she's done."

Lily glared at him. "According to everything I've learned about this town, I should be able to trust her more than I trusted you. She's a Crawford. That means, regardless of what she's done, she's family. This is where she belongs, problems and all. With us. Her family." Even as she said the words, Lily knew they weren't completely reasonable, but she was angry and hurt. "I can't believe I'm saying this sentence out loud, but I believe the ghosts made her do it."

"They did," Polly answered. "She's a butter

pickle now. We'll shut her door tight, so the ghosts can't sneak back inside."

"Besides," Lily gave Mara a pointed look, "if she gets out of line, I'll whammy her again with my powers."

There was no way Lily could back that threat up. She had no way of knowing how to control her powers, but Mara didn't need to know that.

"How do you know I don't have powers to whammy you back?" Mara glanced to where Polly and Dante were discussing floral wedding arrangements to match the siblings' names. "Just because we're talking doesn't mean anything has changed."

"I know because you wouldn't have tried to stop the angry miners from hurting me." Lily lifted her hand like she was carrying an invisible ball. "Now, are you going to behave, or do I subdue you?"

Thankfully, Mara didn't call her on the threat.

Mara kicked her feet. "I didn't want you hurt. I wanted to scare you off. It's safer if you leave."

"Scare me off? You and everyone else in this town. Take a number." Lily arched a brow at Nolan and pursed her lips in irritation.

"You need to let me explain what happened,"

Nolan insisted. "Please, can't we go somewhere and talk?"

"That's so cool," Dante declared. "Look. The deputy is turning a pretty shade of green."

It was then that Lily realized the deputy had stopped talking and merely stood in place. Green scales tipped with yellow covered half her face, moved down under her shirt and reappeared on her hand.

"Crap," Nolan swore, rushing to Herczeg. "She came to ask for help. Echidna bit her last night. I didn't know it was this bad."

"Wow. Snake lady came out of her cave?" Mara said. "I haven't heard of her appearing since I was a kid. Her venom has to be potent after all this time."

"Polly, do you know of a spell or potion that can help?" Nolan asked.

"Dig a hole and bury her," Polly said without hesitation. "Nothing else to be done."

The deputy mumbled, but the words were incoherent.

Nolan ran his hands through his hair and turned pleading eyes to Lily. "I know she might not deserve it. She hasn't been the most helpful when it comes to what's been happening around here but—"

"She's dying?" Lily strode to the deputy's side. "We should get her to the hospital."

"They can't help. The nurse at the hospital sent her here to seek out magical assistance," Nolan said.

Lily touched the deputy's hand that was still flesh colored. "She's freezing cold."

"Reptiles are cold-blooded," Mara said. "Makes sense, I guess."

"We have to do something." Lily didn't know what that would be though.

"Blankets would work just as well, if they were thick," Mara said.

Lily looked at her in question.

Mara shrugged. "What? I literally grew up listening to ghost stories. The old spirits have been around awhile and know a lot."

"Blankets," Lily repeated.

"I mean, burying was the old way, but you always risk dirt in the lungs. Blankets work just as well. The sunlight is what's causing the venom to react. She needs to be enclosed in darkness and warmth until she sheds this new skin." Mara genuinely looked like she wanted to help. "I'm not sure how long it will take. Could be days. Could be weeks."

Lily nodded. "We can do blankets."

Lily attempted to get the deputy to walk with her, but the woman was frozen in her place.

"I got her." Nolan swept the deputy's stiff body into his arms. "Where?"

"My room," Lily said. "It's the closest with blankets."

Nolan rushed in front of her. His foot bumped a gnome with a short body and particularly tall red hat.

"Thimble," Polly cried, going to pick him up. "Please don't get angry. It was an accident. That big scary wolf didn't mean to."

"Let it go, Polly." Lily pulled the kitchen door open for Nolan as he carried the deputy inside. "No one is buying it. The great gnome army didn't do anything."

"Sure they did. They brought you luck." Polly set Thimble on his feet and adjusted him so he turned forward like his friends. "Gnomes are cute to look at. They make people smile. That happiness sends out energy that produces good luck. See, the gnome army clearly won this battle for you."

"So you admit they're just statues." Lily hurried after Nolan, letting the door slam behind her.

"Yes," Polly yelled after her. "Mostly."

Chapter Twenty-Four

Lily tucked the blankets firmly around the deputy's body as Nolan nailed canvas tarps over the windows to block out the light. When she finished, she studied at the mummy figure on her bed. "I hope this works."

"It will." Mara stood in the doorway. "I give you my word."

"Your word isn't—" Nolan began.

"Nolan." Lily held up her hand. "Stop. Unless you want me to start judging you for going all monster on the full moon, you can't judge Mara for going all possessed when the ghosts used her."

He sighed. "I apologize."

"Come on." Lily reached for Mara, who shrugged back out of the way.

"Where?"

"To pick out a bedroom for you. This one is obviously taken for the time being." Lily glanced to the room Nolan had been staying in. She knew she should kick him out but couldn't bring herself to do it. She gestured to the empty one. "That one is free. Or there are two upstairs. Polly and Dante stay on the third floor."

"Why would you do this after all I've done?" Mara clearly had a hard time trusting anyone. Lily couldn't blame her. "How do you know I won't... *you know*... again?"

"Because I'm going to make sure we do everything we can to stop that from happening again. What you went through as a child..." Lily felt tears come to her eyes. "That should never have happened. I wish more than anything I had known about you. I would have found a way to come here and get you away from her. Everything our mother told you..." Lily shook her head in denial and swiped the moisture as it trailed down her cheeks. "Mom was sick. I don't know if something happened to her, and that led her to do drugs. Or if the drugs caused her to be mentally unwell. Or if she was sick to begin with. I do know that, the way this town acts around anyone with our last name, if people saw the signs, they didn't think to help her."

She took a deep breath. This was hard to talk about.

"Or it was me." Mara hugged her arms to her chest. "You don't know that it wasn't because of me."

"Actually, I do. You're twenty. She showed signs before she was pregnant with you. So you see, her illness wasn't because you were evil and sucked the life out of her. You, Mara, are one of us whether you want to be or not. Welcome to the *I Had Marigold Crawford Goode as a Mother* club. Once you're in, you can never get out."

Lily smiled, trying to make a joke.

"Funny," Mara answered wryly.

"So I'm guessing Mara is short for Amaryllis, but why Edison? Are you married?"

Mara chuckled. "Far from it. Not really a lot of options when the only people you talk to are ghosts. I borrowed it from a childhood friend, Luther Edison III. He used to work in the mines. He's been kind of like a strange father figure to me. You might know him by his nickname, Stan."

"Stan?" Lily couldn't hide her surprise.

"Yeah, well, he grows on you. He was always the nicest to me. All he ever wanted me to do was help him look for his shoe. We never found it though." She glanced toward Lily's bedroom, where the sounds of Nolan hammering canvas came from within. "You know that man in there is madly in love with you, right? I saw it the day we met. Whatever you're fighting about, you should forgive him. He would walk through fire for you."

Lily glanced back. She didn't dare show how much those words gave her joy. "Do you think?"

Mara chuckled. "I'll take the room down here. I'm not sure I can handle being next to Polly." She started to walk to the room, only to stop. "Are you sure she's a relative?"

"Yep. You're related to her." Lily nodded. "She's a Crawford. She was mom's twelfth cousin's sister's daughter once removed and then unremoved's mother's aunt's granddaughter."

Mara frowned. "What's unremoved mean?"

"No clue." Lily laughed before saying seriously, "I'm glad you're here, Mara. We'll figure it all out. I promise. You're safe."

"Pickle, darling," Polly called.

Mara's eyes widened, and she quickly shut the bedroom door to hide.

"Pickle, we need to talk. You're giving Crawford witches a bad name. We have to get started with your reeducation immediately. I will not let you out of my sight until..." Polly paused at the top of the stairs. "Oh, Lily, before I forget. I'm pretty sure that feral black cat hanging around is your familiar. You should work on taming it. It peed on Winks."

"I'll try." Lily really had no great motivation to stop the cat from peeing on the gnomes. Maybe her familiar sensed how annoying she found the little statues. What a good little kitty cat. Lily pointed toward the closed door. "She's in there."

Polly went to the door. "Pickle, I'm coming in."

If she wasn't mistaken, it sounded like a dresser was being slid in front of the door as a blockade.

Polly knocked. "Open the door, pickle."

"Polly, I need you to make sure her vessel door thing stays closed," Lily instructed. "We're counting on you."

Polly nodded. "As easy as canning a cucumber. I'm on it."

Lily felt more than saw Nolan behind her. She didn't say anything as she walked into his bedroom and waited by the window. Dante was lying in the yard surrounded by gnomes, who were also tipped over onto their backs. She could see her brother talking though no other person was around. She really hoped that the knocker's aura-contamination-*whatever* didn't last too long, so she could have her snarky brother back.

Hearing Nolan come in, she moved to sit on the bed. Their eyes met, and she knew in that moment everything she needed to. It was the same way she knew Mara just needed a little time, family love, a couple of binding potions... and maybe some therapy. In all honesty, it was better to keep her newly found sister where she could see her. It's not like Lily could send her back out to the mining camp to get turned into a ghost hotel again.

"Tell me," she said to Nolan now they were alone. "Tell me and I'll believe you."

"The council asked me to write up the citations before you came. They also asked me to help nudge you out of town. I said yes." Nolan's eyes turned toward the floor. "It was before you arrived. I thought Goodes coming to Lucky Valley was a bad thing. I—"

"Pickle, I will break down this door," Polly warned.

Nolan again tried to speak and was cut off. "I—"

"Open up and take your medicine like a good girl," Polly ordered.

"One second." Lily lifted her hand and

gently tried to close Nolan's door using magic. The wood slammed hard, and the frame cracked. She jumped in surprise. "Oops."

"A little less next time, dear," Polly yelled, "but good effort."

"I can fix that," Nolan said.

"You were saying." Lily gestured that he should continue.

I thought it was my duty to do what the council asked of me. But then I met you, and in that first moment, everything changed. I wanted you to stay. I wanted—"

"You wanted what?" She stood, needing him to finish what he was saying.

"I wanted you, Lily. From the first moment I saw you laugh in the lawyer's office at one of your brother's jokes. The sound filled me, and I honestly thought you were casting a spell."

"I didn't have my powers then." She took a step toward him.

"I know that now." His eyes again lifted, the soulful dark gaze drawing her in as it always did.

"And I now know that it was Mara trying to scare us, not you. I know you don't like her, but she's my sister. She needs her family. She needs to be around someone who understands what it was like to have a mother like we had."

"It's not that I don't like her. I just sensed her

intentions weren't completely honorable when we met her." Nolan closed some of the distance between them. "Call it my werewolf sixth sense."

"As annoying as it is, I also kind of like you trying to protect me." She closed the distance between them. "I always want there to be complete honesty between us, so I have a confession."

"What?" He looked worried.

"I wasn't sad to see wolf-Nolan tear up that teal couch. It was ugly." Lily pressed her lips together and tried not to laugh.

"I'd planned on giving you a citation for too many garden gnomes," he answered. "I'm pretty sure you can't have a gnomery in city limits without a special permit."

"You can try but Polly will only invite more out of defiance." Lily felt joy erupting through her very being. She knew in that instant she had finally found a home. "When you move in here permanently, that couch is not coming with you."

"What do you mean, when I move in?" He lifted a hand to touch her cheek.

"Oh, I'm sorry, I forgot to tell you an important part of my plan." She batted her lashes at him.

"What part is that?" He glanced at her mouth, leaning ever so slightly forward.

"The part where I say I love you, and I want you to move in here with me and my crazy family, and we get Jesse to come help open a bed and breakfast named after chubby statues." Lily lifted up on her toes so her lips brushed his.

"I didn't hear anything past 'I love you,'" he whispered. "I love you, too, Lily."

Their lips met, and she felt her powers swirling around them, encasing them with love and protection. Nolan lifted her off the floor and carried her toward the bed. As he gently laid her down, she knew that this was everything she could ever want. Forever.

The End

Want more cozy mysteries from Michelle M. Pillow?

Be sure to watch for books from Michelle M. Pillow! Sign up for her newsletter today so you don't miss out on (Un)Lucky Valley books!

Want more of the lovable Polly?

She appeared in these Happily Everlasting Series Books:

Fooled Around and Spelled in Love
by Michelle M. Pillow

Curses and Cupcakes
by Michelle M. Pillow

Once Hunted, Twice Shy
by Mandy M. Roth

Total Eclipse of The Hunt
by Mandy M. Roth

Magick, Mischief, & Kilts!

If you enjoyed this book by Michelle M. Pillow, check out the magically mischievous, modern-day Scottish, paranormal romance series:

Warlocks MacGregor
Love Potions
Spellbound
Stirring Up Trouble
Cauldrons and Confession
Spirits and Spells
More Coming Soon

MichellePillow.com

Newsletter

To stay informed about when a new book in the series installments is released, sign up for updates:

Sign up for Michelle's Newsletter

michellepillow.com/author-updates

About the Author

New York Times & USA TODAY Bestselling Author

Michelle loves to travel and try new things, whether it's a paranormal investigation of an old Vaudeville Theatre or climbing Mayan temples in Belize. She's addicted to movies and used to drive her mother crazy while quoting random scenes with her brother. Though it has yet to happen, her dream is to be a zombie in a horror movie. For the most part she can be found writing in her office with a cup of coffee while wearing pajama pants.

She loves to hear from readers. They can contact her through her website.

www.MichellePillow.com
Facebook: facebook.com/AuthorMichellePillow
Twitter: @michellepillow

Featured Titles from Michelle M. Pillow

Magical Scottish Contemporary Romances

Warlocks MacGregor
Love Potions
Spellbound
Stirring Up Trouble
Cauldrons and Confession
Spirits and Spells
More Coming Soon

Paranormal Shapeshifter Romances

Dragon Lords Series

Barbarian Prince

Perfect Prince

Dark Prince

Warrior Prince

His Highness The Duke

The Stubborn Lord

The Reluctant Lord

The Impatient Lord

The Dragon's Queen

Lords of the Var Series

The Savage King

The Playful Prince

The Bound Prince

The Rogue Prince

The Pirate Prince

Captured by a Dragon-Shifter Series

Determined Prince

Rebellious Prince

Stranded with the Cajun

Hunted by the Dragon

Mischievous Prince
Headstrong Prince

Futuristic Space Pirate Romance

Space Lords Series

His Frost Maiden
His Fire Maiden
His Metal Maiden
His Earth Maiden
His Wood Maiden

To learn more about the Dragon Lords World series of books and to stay up to date on the latest book list visit www.MichellePillow.com

Complimentary Material

CHECK OUT THE EXCERPTS BEFORE YOU BUY!

Fooled Around and Spelled in Love

A HAPPILY EVERLASTING SERIES NOVEL

Welcome to Everlasting, Maine, where there's no such thing as normal.

Anna Crawford is well aware her town is filled with supernaturals, but she isn't exactly willing to embrace her paranormal gifts. Her aunt says she's a witch-in-denial. All Anna wants is to live a quiet "normal" life and run her business, Witch's Brew Coffee Shop and Bakery. But everything is about to be turned upside down the moment Jackson Argent walks into her life.

Jackson isn't sure why he agreed to come back to his boyhood home of Everlasting. It's like a spell was cast and he couldn't say no. Covering the Cranberry Festival isn't exactly the hard-hitting news this reporter is used to. But when a local death is ruled an accident, and the police aren't interested in investigating, he takes it upon himself to get to the bottom of the mystery. To do that, he'll need to enlist the help of the beautiful coffee shop owner.

It soon becomes apparent things are not what they seem and more than coffee is brewing in Everlasting.

Fooled Around and Spelled in Love
by Michelle M. Pillow

Curses and Cupcakes

A HAPPILY EVERLASTING SERIES NOVEL

Welcome to Everlasting, Maine, where there's no such thing as normal.

Marcy Lewis is cursed (honestly and truly) which makes dating very interesting. With a string of loser boyfriends behind her, she's done looking for love in all the wrong places. That is until the new firefighter arrives in the sleepy seaside town of Everlasting. Nicholas Logan is unlike any other man she's ever had in her life. When someone starts sending her photographs that raise a red flag it soon becomes apparent that she's not just cursed, she's in serious danger.

Nicholas doesn't know what to make of the charismatic young woman managing the local coffee shop. As a string of mysterious fires begin popping up around town, the two unite in search of clues as to who or what is responsible, discovering along the way that things are very rarely what they seem to be.

Curses and Cupcakes
by Michelle M. Pillow

Love Potions (Warlocks MacGregor)

BY MICHELLE M. PILLOW

Contemporary Paranormal Scottish Warlocks

A little magickal mischief never hurt anyone…

Erik MacGregor, from a clan of ancient Scottish warlocks, isn't looking for love. After centuries, it's not even a consideration…until he moves in next door to Lydia Barratt. It's clear that the shy beauty wants nothing to do with him, but he's drawn to her nonetheless and determined to win her over.

Lydia Barratt just wants to be left alone to grow flowers and make lotions in her old Victorian house. The last thing she needs is a demanding Scottish man meddling in her private life. Just because he's gorgeous and totally rocks a kilt doesn't mean she's going to fall for his seductive manner.

But Erik won't give up and just as Lydia let's her guard down, his sister decides to get involved. Her little love potion prank goes terribly wrong, making Lydia the target of his sudden embarrassingly obsessive behavior. They'll have to find a way to pull Erik out of the spell fast when it becomes clear that Lydia has more than a lovesick warlock to worry about. Evil lurks within the shadows and it plans to use Lydia, alive or dead, to take out Erik and his clan for good.

Love Potions Excerpt

"Ly-di-ah! I sit beneath your window, laaaass, singing 'cause I loooove your a—"

"For the love of St. Francis of Assisi, someone call a vet. There is an injured animal screaming in pain outside," Charlotte interrupted the flow of music in ill-humor.

Lydia lifted her forehead from the kitchen table. Her windows and doors were all locked, and yet Erik's endlessly verbose singing penetrated the barrier of glass and wood with ease.

Charlotte held her head and blinked heavily.

Her red-rimmed eyes were filled with the all too poignant look of a hangover. She took a seat at the table and laid her head down. Her moan sounded something like, "I'm never moving again."

"You need fluids," Lydia prescribed, getting up to pour unsweetened herbal tea from the pitcher in the fridge. She'd mixed it especially for her friend. It was Gramma Annabelle's hangover recipe of willow bark, peppermint, carrot, and ginger. The old lady always had a fresh supply of it in the house while she was alive. Apparently, being a natural witch also meant in partaking in natural liquors. Annabelle had kept a steady supply of moonshine stashed in the basement. If the concert didn't stop soon she might try to find an old bottle.

"*Ly-di-ah!*"

"Omigod. Kill me," Charlotte moaned. "No. Kill him. Then kill me."

"*Ly-di-ah!*"

Erik had been singing for over an hour. At first, he'd tried to come inside. She'd not invited him and the barrier spell sent him sprawling back into the yard. He didn't seem to mind as he found a seat on some landscaping timbers and began his serenade. The last time she'd asked him to be quiet, he'd gotten louder and overly enthusiastic. In fact, she'd been too scared to pull back the curtains for a clearer look, but she was pretty sure he'd been dancing on her lawn, shaking his kilt.

"Omigod," Charlotte muttered, pushing up and angrily going to a window. Then grimacing, she said, "Is he wearing a tux jacket with his kilt?"

"Don't let him see you," Lydia cried out in a panic. It was too late. The song began with renewed force.

"He's…" Charlotte frowned. "I think it's dancing."

Since the damage was done, Lydia joined Charlotte at the window. Erik grinned. He lifted his arms to the side and kicked his legs, bouncing around the yard like a kid on too much sugar. "Maybe it's a traditional Scottish dance?"

Both women tilted their heads in unison as his kilt kicked up to show his perfectly formed ass.

"He's not wearing…" Charlotte began.

"I know. He doesn't," Lydia answered. Damn, the man had a fine body. Too bad Malina's trick had turned him insane.

To find out more about Michelle's books visit www.MichellePillow.com

77727555R00201

Made in the USA
Middletown, DE
25 June 2018